NERVOUS SYSTEM

Also by Lina Meruane, available in English

Seeing Red
Viral Voyages: Tracing AIDS in Latin America

NERVOUS SYSTEM

A NOVEL

Lina Meruane

*Translated from the Spanish by
Megan McDowell*

Graywolf Press

Originally published in 2018 as *Sistema nervioso* by Penguin Random House
Grupo Editorial, Santiago.

This publication is made possible, in part, by the voters of Minnesota through
a Minnesota State Arts Board Operating Support grant, thanks to a legisla-
tive appropriation from the arts and cultural heritage fund. Significant support has also been provided by Target Foundation, the McKnight Foundation,
the Lannan Foundation, the Amazon Literary Partnership, and other gener-
ous contributions from foundations, corporations, and individuals. To these
organizations and individuals we offer our heartfelt thanks.

MINNESOTA
STATE ARTS BOARD

CLEAN
WATER
LAND &
LEGACY
AMENDMENT

Published by Graywolf Press
250 Third Avenue North, Suite 600
Minneapolis, Minnesota 55401

www.graywolfpress.org

Published in the United States of America

ISBN 978-1-64445-055-0

2 4 6 8 9 7 5 3 1
First Graywolf Printing, 2021

Library of Congress Control Number: 2020944192

Cover design: Kimberly Glyder

Cover image: lekcej, iStock / Getty Images Plus

To my brothers in orbit.

A system has not just one history but every possible history.

Stephen Hawking on Richard Feynman

contents

NERVOUS SYSTEM

black holes

The country went dark. One giant black hole, no candles.

In another time, another place, her house had been full of *long skinny nebulous* candles, wrapped in blue paper or tied with string, kept for emergencies.

There were no candles in the country of the present, where the electricity never went out. Never, until it did.

Ella watched as the lamp that half lit her face and scarcely lit the night died. She sat for a moment with her hands hovering over the keyboard, blinking in the light of a screen full of numbers. Ella. She. Wondering whether a fuse had blown. Whether it was just a simple blackout or an attack on the old nuclear power station built and abandoned during the Cold War. Not too far from her building, atomic energy that could explode any minute now.

Forever on the verge of catastrophe, her country of the past used to suffer power outages from floods, or from snow falling on trees and from branches onto electrical posts. Exposed cables electrocuting the wind. Ditches and rivers overflowing. And buildings that shuddered from the constant grinding of subterranean plates. Volcanoes crackled, spraying lava. Forests burned, trees fell, scorched to their roots, houses to their foundations, the *signs roads hives melted*, birds flapping. Their bodies charred if they didn't get out fast enough.

Those bodies, possessed by the light.

* * *

This is going to slow me down, Ella cried, throwing up her arms. More, it's going to slow me down even more, and she howled at El. He. To El, who had surely already heard her in some corner, slamming drawers, searching in vain for a flashlight. She rummaged through papers and keys and she cursed. El's inflammatory voice rose to tell her, stop that, Electron. It was the same thing he'd been saying to her for months, that she should shut her computer, disavow her doctoral thesis and the anxiety brought on by the life sentence of a project like that.

Working such long hours could set her off. That's what El said, and he knew about explosions. But he didn't say explode and he didn't say collapse. He said, burning his tongue on a fresh cup of coffee he was now balancing in the dark. As though spitting, he said, short-circuit.

And Ella saw a quick spark traverse his nerves. His skin covered with hairs, *ignited vibrating electric.*

* * *

4

Now even the most indistinct, insignificant stars spattered the night with their light. They seemed to give off smoke, fiery above the extinguished city. Ella paused at the window to admire them. The radiant constellations, the pulverized physical universe that she couldn't manage to capture in the dissertation she'd been writing for years. Years without writing. She'd started out studying elliptical orbits and their magnetic fields, the asteroid belts and the remains of millenary supernovas; she'd spent months or maybe even years on the star systems closest to the sun, searching in vain for habitable planets, and she hypothesized the positions of celestial bodies similar to earth. One thing led to another, each refuting the one before, obliging her to start her research all over again.

This final attempt would be spent on stars that had already lost their light and collapsed in on themselves, forming dense black holes.

Except those holes needed an adviser who knew all about them and was willing to guide her dissertation. One who believed Ella was prepared to deal with such density. But not even Ella was sure she could do it, and time was running out.

* * *

And then the bulbs all came on simultaneously, as though electrified by lightning. Reactivated after an interval of hours. Ella opened a can of coke, loaded with sugar and caffeine—she would drink to her own detriment before sinking once more into the screen. She would calculate figures of cosmic deviation and radiation. She would measure the movement of the stars stretched out around the *spinning greedy point-of-no-return* black hole that would soon swallow them. And she'd type formulas she would later proceed to disprove.

5

El would see her appear in the doorway, that morning and the ones to come, and the scar across his forehead would wrinkle. Ella would understand that he, too, had stopped believing she could finish.

*   *   *

It was while thinking about blackouts and bottomless holes that the desire to get sick ignited in her. Ella considered it but couldn't decide on an illness. A cold or a flu wouldn't give her the time she needed to finish the thesis. Pneumonia would keep her from working. Cancer was too risky. Then her memory turned to her Father's bleeding ulcer, which had kept him bedridden for several months: she imagined herself lying in a different bed, computer on her lap, eating poached eggs and insipid crackers and taking irritating sips of coca-cola on the sly.

To fall ill: Ella would ask the favor of her birth mother, her deceased genetic mother. The one she never met. Ella always invoked her when things got hard. Lighting a stick of incense, she begged her mother to infect her with something serious but transitory. Not to die like the mother herself, suddenly. Just enough to take one semester off, to not have to teach all those planetary sciences classes to so many distracted students whom she had to *instruct evaluate forget immediately.* Just a brief reprieve from that poorly paid job so she could dedicate herself fully to another job that paid nothing at all.

Ella had no one else to ask. Her Father had already given all he had.

*   *   *

Secret-pact story. No one knew the Father had funded her studies in the country of the present with savings for his future old age.

6

Ella's three siblings and that Mother who wasn't hers had been left out of their mutual agreement. Because the Mother who came to fill in for the first would never have allowed it. All that money! she would have cried in defense of her disinherited twins. It's a fortune! she would argue, fearing the indignities the expense could entail for the Father.

The Father would never have told his second wife that this was the promise he'd made to the first, in critical condition after her daughter's birth. Promise me Ella will study what she wants, that you'll pay for whatever program she chooses without any conditions, the first wife murmured in a voice that wavered but knew death was coming. It's what I would have wanted. What I would have done. Study. If I hadn't, and she stopped, closed her eyes a long second. Gotten married, she said, the words coming unstrung. So young, to you. What I would have.

* * *

El, hair combed, face freshly shaved, already finishing breakfast, ready to head off to the carbon laboratory to date some newly dusted bones. Ella, dressed but unkempt, dragged herself into the bedroom to choose her teacher's uniform and assemble her notes for the five classes she would teach that day in three different city schools. Dull-eyed, she sat down at the table and confided in El what she wanted. To get sick. To have six months free. To stay home alone with her two hands, the eighty-two keys under ten fingers tapping intermittently. To leave her fingerprints on a thesis that was missing arduous weeks of work.

Be careful what you wish for, is what El replied in his language, the language of Ella's present, knitting his brows into a single line. His sharp nose pointed to the empty plate as he murmured his warning. You don't need your dad's approval, he said with a weary air, you don't even need to tell him you haven't finished, that you might not ever finish. You don't need that degree, Electronica, not to teach astronomy classes. Extraterrestrial planetary sciences, corrects Ella.

Ella hadn't admitted to El that she never had a scholarship, or told him where all that money, down to the last red cent, had really come from, from whose pocket, nor had she told him she'd just called her Father to tell him, I've defended, dad, I'm a doctor now. Or that her Father replied sadly or perhaps resentfully that it was about time, *hija*. That her Father had fallen silent before informing her that she was now the only real doctor in the family. A doctor in the true sense of the word, murmured her Father, while Ella's throat tightened.

Ella didn't know why she'd lied, but that, too, was a lie.

* * *

Be careful, and El got up from the table and left without saying goodbye.

Nine weeks, sixty-three days, 1,512 hours later, Ella was still the lackluster inhabitant of that apartment where, more than live with El, eat with El, sleep with El, entwine her legs with his until their bodies blended together, she shut herself away to work. The exams had been corrected, her students assigned grades. She'd finished the semester without a sneeze, without a migraine, but now summer was starting and time was entirely her own again, and she would work without interruption.

And Ella typed, yes, but then she stopped, she got distracted, wrote text messages full of typos, found excluded terms in lists, jotted down unconnected words that rhymed but were useless to her, in spite of their strange beauty. And she bit a nail until it bled, or scratched her leg and made a cup of tea with milk and peered out the window and then went back to her chair.

* * *

Lean back, stretch both arms. Bend a stiff neck forward and to one side. A sudden cramp shoots down the spine and then, stillness.

* * *

In that hot, wet summer there was only the anguished breeze from an ancient fan.

Rushed notches numbers on the wall as days and hours passed. 1,564. 1,598. 1,613. And in all those hours Ella still didn't move, an electric pillow propped under her neck. Cursed be the too-high table, the hard chair that now forced her into a horizontal position. Cursed be the stabbing pain every time she changed position.

Two more days and I'll go back to work, Ella decreed, turning up the current as high as it would go.

* * *

To have wanted to burn. Both hands suspended in the air, Ella had raised the small can of kerosene and gulped it down. The body that was hers at five years old didn't retain the flavor of the fuel her Grandmother used to stir up orange and blue flames in the fireplace.

She couldn't recall what happened next.

* * *

Turning off the electric pillow and getting out of bed, Ella thought about first-degree burns: an unbearable stinging had settled into her *shoulder neck ember*. Sitting at her computer, she felt an invisible wound wrapping her up and suffocating her. The summer was still reheating the bricks outside, and Ella, who burst into flames when she moved, who died on getting dressed, decided to work naked in the kitchen.

Only the spinning blades on the ceiling soothed the burning.

The only thing that mattered now was the bonfire in her shoulder.

* * *

Had she sought out the burn, or had she mistakenly put her hand through the grate that protected the scorching burner of the stove? The mark left by that deliberate childhood accident is now just a faded spot on her skin, a scar that back then must have covered the entire back of her hand.

* * *

Inflammatio. In flames. *En llamas*. Ardor without romance.

The ancient philosopher of inflammation had grown cold twenty centuries ago and lay stiff underground. But he couldn't be lying there, not stiff or dressed or naked, Ella thought, but disintegrated and scattered beneath the ruins. El had explained it to her; he was her bone expert: there would be nothing left of that cadaver, not a splinter or a gram of *brain sweat chest hair*. Only calcium and phosphorus. And hydrogen atoms, Ella said, molecules. That body would no longer be exposed to the slightest possibility of inflammation, which, as the same thinker had described, was distinguished by four basic principles.

Rubor. Calor. Dolor. Tumor.

Those were the signs Ella had looked for on her own back, angling a mirror between her shoulder blade and clavicle. It wasn't red. Not swollen or hot to the touch. There was no trace of damage, but the pain was like another skin.

* * *

Instead of dialing her Father it was El she called, to share the burning enigma with him. There was no sign she'd burned herself. It's not even red but it hurts, Ella explained, as she spread toothpaste over *lumbar torso dead tongues*. But El knew only about desiccated bones. I don't know what to tell you, and his voice sounded distracted, or maybe hostile. He couldn't help her from the remote country where he was attending a conference, but she went on talking as though to herself, holding the phone with pasty fingers. I must have burned myself on the inside, underneath, it's the only explanation I can think of.

El had warned her. Too many hours working. Too many all-nighters and whole days of electric heat on a muscle. Too much abandonment of what they had once been. But he didn't say it again. Ask your Father, he said instead.

* * *

And that's how the summer gradually dies. Like that, grudging, half-dressed, and smelling of menthol, not a single line further in the manuscript, resolved to abandon her thesis until the burning subsides, she gets on a plane to meet El in the remote conference country.

That remote, provincial city, so damp and fresh, so shaken by nocturnal winds, is a relief.

And though the burn and its ghost persist, their intensity wanes. The anxiety eases, but between Ella and her symptom something else settles in: a slight numbness that starts in the shoulder and extends along the arm to the elbow until it reaches the back of her right hand, the fingers where it all started.

That was just speculation—maybe it didn't start there. Her defective shoulder blade and arm allowed for other readings. Because now it wasn't just *shoulder arm carpal tunnel* but also the base of her skull, the edge of her face, her tongue.

Under the warm shower at the hotel where they're staying, Ella notices her skin has faded away. She touches it but feels nothing. The towel slides like a breeze over her back.

And when El touches her, what does he feel? But it's been a long time since he touched her. When he looks at her, does he see her disappearing?

* * *

Ella typed *arm falling asleep* in her search bar, and then she couldn't fall asleep.

She wrote to a neurologist in the land of the present but he was the kind of doctor who was stingy with words, replying in monosyllables when he even remembered to respond to her messages. Then she turned to her Father, even though numb, sleeping arms weren't his specialty, and the Father said over the phone, from the antipodes of the past, that it didn't seem necessary to rush back for a case of paresthesia. The neurologist agreed, in a laconic, unpunctuated line sent in the future tense, that a pinched nerve was no cause for alarm. But her Father's opinion, in another call to the remote country, was that it couldn't be a pinched nerve. The Mother's opinion was the same. Ella's first-born brother cracked his knuckles. No one consulted the other siblings.

Only El stayed nervously silent.

* * *

And the woman Ella has called Mother ever since she met her is the one who sends text messages every morning to ask about the arm where that strange sleep is spreading. And Ella writes back with a brief report: *no change, no news.* And signing off to that Mother who is hers but not, she types: *thanks for checking in, I arm fine!* Only after she sends her message does she notice that her dyslexic fingers have injected an *r.*

* * *

Portrait of a rebellious arm leaning against the elevator doors every time they came up from the parking garage. Don't lean on that, it's dangerous, warned her Father, but Ella rested the weight of her childhood on those rusty doors that slid back over themselves, screeching. The steel sheets opened at the sixth floor and caught her jacket sleeve, her soft muscles, her humerus bone. And the stuck doors and the Mother *screaming roaring goat bellows*, afraid her arm would be separated from her body, when the Father grasped hold of her with his giant hands and yanked her out.

Her Father gave her an unforgettable beating that Ella has, nevertheless, forgotten.

The daughter sitting on the Father's lap. The daughter drying her eyes while her Father tells her a story that she has also forgotten. So many moments are asleep in her memory.

This is her forced vacation in a remote country. It's always worse in the afternoons.

Waiting for the doctor that the hotel has called for Ella, they both order soup and sip it stealthily in the lobby. Again and again they look up from their bowls to see if he's arrived, but the doctor walks right past them like a ghost stripped of his sheet, then leaves without ever seeing them.

They'll have to wait until he finishes his evening rounds, wait for him to return for the lost arm and it's already noon. Bells ringing from the church towers.

* * *

The doctor was named after a soccer player, but his examination style was more like that of a trainer or masseuse. He asked her to perform a series of coordinated movements in the small hotel room. Walk forward and back, in a straight line. Lift her arms while he pressed down on them to measure her strength. Touch the tip of her nose with one index finger and then the other, follow his finger as it traced a horizontal line in the air. He put a knuckle between each pair of vertebrae and asked if it hurt, he palpated her head in search of bumps, he twisted her neck as she let it go limp. He blew on her toes after touching them with a pin. He couldn't reach a diagnosis. Maybe it was a nerve pinched by a disk, he said, indecisive, but we'd have to get an x-ray.

Tapping the table with just-trimmed nails, the Father waits as his daughter relays the doctor's verdict from the remote country. He insists on talking to the doctor himself, and the two of them discuss her fate, which will be worse if the Father is right. The masseuse-doctor prescribes an injection that the Father vetoes, and the discredited doctor shrugs his shoulders and gives up, backs off, returns the receiver with her Father inside.

It's not a strangled nerve, insists the impatient Father at the other end of the line. That nerve's path doesn't match your symptoms. And in the deep voice of the professor he has also been, he merely starts listing the signs that would indicate a brain hemorrhage or tumor.

* * *

Between the remote hotel sheets, Ella rubs the numbed edge of her face as if she could wake it up. Her eye wanders again over medical websites that link paresthesia to diseases that end in paralysis. The eye rolls, falls out, hits the keyboard, and wakes El, who grunts, please, turn that off.

El takes her cold hand, interlaces one finger with another finger *stiff magnetic under the weather* until he catches them all. The rough skin that unites and abrades them. The index finger that shuts off the light. The wrist that bends. The palm of the hand that covers her eyelids and keeps her from reading.

Those websites that her Father categorically forbade her. But up till now, out of all of them, the doctor she's ignored the most has been her Father.

* * *

Back in the city of the present, the neurologist sits with Ella's fingers between his own; they are fragile, cold, as if rather than holding her hand, he were looking for a pulse.

15

That doctor will decree punished vertebrae and a nerve crushed by excess work or all the papers that she carries on *ramps bridges trains city skeletons*. And that tingling in her face—is she perhaps nervous? The doctor unfurls an involuntary smile, inappropriate, unbearable, a convulsive smile: your nervous face. Nerves or nervousness, who knows? No one knows, Ella thinks. The neurologist should know, but he's a prejudiced doctor. I'm a woman, but that doesn't make me crazy. That thought radiates through her cheeks and spatters her tongue. Could be it's not a pinched nerve, Ella emphasizes, emulating her Father. It *is* a nerve, replies the doctor, loudly underlining the verb. Could we check, just to be sure? Ella asks, following, in plural, the suggestion of the doctor or masseuse back in the remote country. We're completely sure, Ella sees the neurologist say, rubbing his eyelids under bushy brows, absolutely sure, that's what he's saying, drawing out the *u* in his absoluteness and his surety. Unless you insist, and he pauses to size her up, the doctor gnashing his polished teeth before Ella, who insists, I would absolutely insist, hiding her crooked teeth, the molars full of cavities worried by her tongue.

We know exactly what the images will show, the doctor proclaims, rising victoriously from his chair, his duplicate fingers typing up the order for the MRI.

* * *

To orient themselves as they plunge into the night, bats emit hundreds of cries, at different frequencies, which bounce back to report on all that moves in the area. Everything this blind creature cannot see takes on shape, volume. Resonance, echo, is medicine's blind howl. A sonorous ray of images in the body's impenetrable darkness.

* * *

Ella had never been in the echo chamber. The Mother, who *has* gone through it, recommends that she close her eyes and try to focus on something pleasant. Surrounded, though, by the grape-shot of shrill beeps and the peals of exasperating bells, Ella can't manage to find a single soothing place to take refuge. Bad memories assail her. The call informing her of the attack at El's excavation. El's head, *all bandaged full of silence*, and hers, full of fear. She's besieged by imaginary radioactive stations—bombs made of the same hydrogen that lights the stars—with pigeons shitting oxide all over them. Her investigation full of holes that she doesn't know how to fill. Perhaps she'll have to live with that, Ella thinks, die with that, kill someone with that—her Father, always on the verge of collapse.

Suddenly, the beeping of the machine changes, softens, speeds up, and she's seized by a wind, relentless as the resonant chamber she's inside. Waves rise up against rocks while Ella sinks down into the ocean, letting the current carry her out to sea. She is swimming in the sound, crossing or trying to cross a turbulent southern strait where so many scurvy-filled sailors ran aground, so many *ships masts rodents of conquest*. The ocean rears up, curves into a foamy crest, lifts, and drops her in a crash of hardened water. Her ears are stopped up as she moves through thunderous upswellings, focuses on her breathing. Almost there, she tells herself, exhausted, inhaling and exhaling without losing the rhythm, almost to the shore, she tells herself, filling her mouth with air and salty water, swallowing the ocean whole again and again, and again.

* * *

That day at the beach. Ella's Cousin pressuring her to go into a choppy, forbidden sea. The signs forbade swimming but the close Cousin, who was older and more daring, more insolent, a ring in her belly button, hair streaked by the sun—a Cousin who would do everything in life ahead of time, *love marriage children widowhood—* that Cousin insisted Ella get in the water. Don't be such a baby, collecting all your little shells. And seeing Ella hesitate with her jar of empty shells in hand, the Cousin opened her mouth and offered her a candy, already sucked on but still whole, pineapple flavor. Ella took the sweet and put it on her own tongue like a scapular, and she stripped off her fear, tempted by the smiling Cousin in her bikini. They left their towels on the sand and ran into *cold water crystal needles* that made their bones ache. And they swam out, dragged along by the current and the whirlpools and the high concave waves on their way to breaking. That hand-to-hand combat drained them, the heaving crests came three at a time and fell, stirring the shining foam and opening sinkholes in the sea floor. The waves multiplied, determined to defeat them. And then the Cousin, stripped now of her audacity, signaled that she wanted to get out. She took a couple of strokes before standing up and then a couple of firm steps, but lost her footing in an unexpected hole and lost her head, lost control of her whole body. Ella saw the Cousin sink and emerge and grunt with her seaweed-black mouth, I'm drowning, and disappear again. And for a moment her head reappeared, her blond hair bedraggled and a pair of fixed doll's eyes shining with salt. Ella screamed to her, but they were drenched screams that sank with the Cousin, don't be dumb, Ella howled, and she thought: it's the moon raising the tide, mixing up the waves, it's the same choppy sea as always with its *knotty medusas jellyfish seaweed*, as though reciting a spell. And Ella came up from behind, put an arm under the Cousin's shoulders, and slowly towed her in. Her skinny legs struggled to propel them both, her arms trying to keep the Cousin's almost dead weight from dragging them to the bottom. Both of them.

Ella cursed that Cousin as she lay on the beach, still in her bikini now green with seaweed, still shivering, still coughing. The Cousin clearing bits of ocean from her lungs. Ella cursed her loudly until her voice broke, and, mute, she began to kick *shells burning sand go to hells* at her Cousin.

* * *

Portrait of the massive hole in the center of the galaxy. It's a navel so dark no one has ever seen it. It can be intuited only because we can see how fluorescent stars and clouds of gas are pulled toward that *elliptical perilous periscope spiral* that consumes all. A body that approaches its edge will stretch and redden until it disappears, devoured by the hole. That's what Ella was thinking about when the resonant machine fell silent. The technician extracted her from the box that was more like a giant tube, and, taking out her ear plugs, he said, it wasn't so bad in there, right? and Ella shook her head, but the technician must have thought she'd come unhinged when he heard her reply, no, not too bad, but of course it wouldn't be, a body wouldn't know when it was falling into a cosmic whirlpool, it would go on navigating blindly, and the distant echo of the tideless sea would distract it from the sounds of its own agony.

* * *

The days pass like spiky ocean waves. The wait is her vertigo now.

Finally the telephone vibrates and emits two reports as curt as her doctor. Positive: none of her vertebrae are squeezing any of her nerves. Negative: something of another sort has become visible inside her spine. Just what sort of something? Ella asks, collapsing into a chair in the classroom where she's just finished teaching. Inflammation in the spinal cord. A strident white stain in the neck. But instead of making an appointment to show her, the neurologist sends her back, headfirst, into the radioactive box.

* * *

And while they're setting up her appointment for another MRI, her Father suggests Ella ask for a copy of the last one. She walks over to the neurological institute to ask for her images, and as she goes down the stairs to the basement and waits for them, a memory lights up inside her: the cancer that her Mother had survived a decade before, along with the scene in a novel Ella read while the Mother was recovering. It's the image of a woman very different from the Mother, and at the same time just as sick or maybe more so, though they'll find out only later just how sick they are. Sitting in the rickety chair in the basement, Ella sees the woman in the novel gazing at the films of her illness taped to the bathroom mirror like dirty rags hung up to dry. Two black rags marbled with radiographic white. In the blotches of her chest the woman glimpses the face of the virgin who will save her. More like the virgin who'll carry her to hell, Ella thinks, knowing how the novel ends.

Ella still hasn't been visited by virgins or demons, because she still hasn't seen anything, hasn't peered inside herself. The translucent slices of her spine are encrypted on the disk they hand her now, along with a printed report that she'll have to *decipher interpret cerebral circuits*, word by word.

The weight of each word is gravity's pull.

Spinal medulla médula, from the ancient *myelós*. The signal from Ella's spinal cord is not good and demyelination is the destruction of the myelin that protects the nerve. *Myelitis mielitis miel mellif- luous*, she slowly repeats, pronouncing that name, so sweet, so bitter, that leaves such a bad taste in her mouth.

* * *

Her Father often says: information is not knowledge. As if Ella didn't know that. Ella, who is full of cosmic data she has no clue how to interpret. Ella, who has passed on planetary knowledge to her students one semester after another without rest, and who now returns to the classroom in spite of her spine.

And because knowledge is not just accumulated, it's also lost if you don't return to it, Ella repeats the material she goes around teaching in the city's schools. Her new students put up more and more resistance to the idea that the universe began with a cosmic explosion, and that ever since the big bang it has continued to expand, tending toward disorder and disintegration.

A broken egg can never recover its previous shape: a classic example from astrophysical speculation that Ella repeats by rote. But one student interrupts to say, then we'll eat that egg scrambled with salt, onions, potatoes, *y un poquito de* our teacher. That broken egg will be recycled because nothing is destroyed, everything is transformed. That's what the chemistry teacher said, the student adds with an insolent smirk. The others laugh at her answer. Ella smiles sadly, reminding herself that those young people still live in the hopeful order of consecutive time, which had never been hers.

Ella came from a galaxy extinguished thousands of millions of years ago.

* * *

Years ago, the epidemic of dictatorship had spread and Ella's Friend had to take refuge in her grandmother's country house, the cold adobe house with no electricity or potable water, with a mud oven in the kitchen and a yard with a chicken coop and mangy dogs. Ella went there on weekends to escape her older brother. The Father, still a widower then, knew it was better to get her out of the apartment, get her out, out of there, and though the house was outside the city he drove Ella down old streets full of potholes and dirt roads, past fallen gates and toppled posts, and he left her with her Friend until Sunday. That way Ella wouldn't be surrounded by the Oriental plane trees she was allergic to, he told himself, and he stopped himself from thinking the things it was better not to think. Ella, his daughter, would get some fresh air. Fruit ripened on trees of iridescent green. Explosive orange persimmons. Lumpy loquats. Fuzzy peaches split open to bare the raw flesh.

His daughter, thought the Father, surrounded by health.

The daughter would discover that chickens blinked backward, and maybe their thoughts were backward too.

If only the Father had known about how the girls picked bluish-green figs from the trees, and instead of washing them only dirtied them in the stream before devouring them. How they leaped across that turbulent creek where her Friend's cousin had fallen. How her aunt and uncle had forded the current only to find him tangled in the underwater weeds. If he'd known about how they jumped that stream with their eyes closed. If he'd known. How they crept into the chicken coop. How they shooed away the roosters and collected warm brown eggs covered in feathers and straw. How they threw the eggs at cars parked on the street, heedless of the price they could pay. They were competing to see who could hit a windshield when they saw the grandmother approaching from a distance. They both stuck the eggs they were holding into the hollow between their legs, hanging in their underwear like testicles, and they stood very still. Act natural, the Friend whispered to Ella. But Ella's was the face of a broken egg, the crunch of shell. That face was *calcium odium ovum cum*, yolk sliding down her leg to the edge of her sock.

An egg that would never recover its previous shape. The shells Ella would gather into a napkin and add to her particle collection.

Instead of sleeping, Ella's Friend crowed over stories about the neighbors and the baker lady, and she got stuck in a stutter talking about her cousins of different ages and dates of demise. And she laughed low at her slow, fat grandmother with her lipstick melted in the heat of her mouth. Her distracted grandmother, so easy to fool. A headless chicken, her grandmother. And Ella's Friend crowed ever louder but she sowed a field of silence around her parents, and Ella intuited that they should be somewhere in the story, if they were still alive. Her Friend's babble was full of silenced voices that drove them both crazy. Ella wanted her Friend to be quiet and get those voices out of her head, those lost parents, the drowned cousin, her own dead mother, her living Father who could die anytime. She covered her ears. Let's sleep, tomorrow you can go on with the story, but the Friend seemed determined to fill the night with her tireless tale-telling. All right, Ella said, finally sitting up on the mattress. Get your things. And the Friend, a future saver of lives, finally stopped talking. The Friend, her hollow-eyed face, her dark childhood. She donned some wool socks, and, carrying blankets, they left the house and went out to the observatory of that starry yard. They chose three shining stars and gave two the names of the absent parents. The cousin's name went to the small star. There they are, Ella said, up in the sky. Space curved around matter. The vibrating universe, the hissing galaxies. The insolent distance of stars. They slept guarded by a milky moon and pastoral constellations. They woke up with the sun in their eyes.

Ella's notebook was that open sky full of comets leaving a wake of *light dust shooting slime*. Her Friend's notebook would be sprinkled with little gold paper stars. Ella would adore and hate her Friend because she would pass all her classes without trying, she would graduate with top grades, the highest GPA, she'd finish her degree and her ER specialization without lying to a soul. Without any parents to lie to.

That was the Friend who was now at the other end of the line. That Friend listened to her without a peep, because there were key pieces missing in the study of the spine and anyway it wasn't her field, though she could look into it. But Ella's Father was already investigating with other doctors from his hospital.

* * *

Ella is turning thirty-nine in another box where she'll have to spend even more time before reemerging into reality. The years fold back, and before her rise the howls she tore from the mother she can't remember, everything so dark, so viscous. She doesn't dare look. She's afraid to open her mouth lest it fill up with fear. The rattle of maternal agony disturbs her, and she's another year older. And there's no one there, no *celulas madre*, no mother nature. No cake or candles or gulps of saltwater. No ocean to cross, only fluid, *amniotic amnesiac assassin*. That placenta like a toxic jellyfish. That taut cord breaking the mother from inside while Ella's own head struggles into the light of a white lamp that blinds her, toward the noise to which she'll add her newborn wail. To be the foreign body that rends and wounds another body that won't stop bleeding. Spending a birthday in that crypt full of inhuman hissing is the curse of the dead mother Ella never should have invoked. She shouldn't have awoken her in the beyond. Shouldn't have asked anything of her. Because, trussed up head to toe as she is, motionless as she must be, with a worn-out panic button between her fingers and a needle driven into her arm, the opaque fluid rising through her veins to impregnate her brain with contrast, because there, there inside, at the end of it all, her conscience is filling up with matricide.

* * *

Ella's hand touched the cord under the bed, tugged on it, and the electric pillow appeared. As if it were a treacherous rat, she lifted

24

it by the tail, disgusted: this was what had made her sick, she was convinced. It had damaged her spine, and still she hadn't been able to take sick leave. She tossed it in the garbage without telling El.

* * *

The living Mother and all the advice she'd hooked the daughter up to. Opinions. Judgments. Convictions. How that guy wasn't good for her because a virus had damaged his spinal cord and atrophied his shin over the fibula. The guy limped with his bony leg in shorts. He danced with her at parties, a little sickly, a little uncoordinated, and he gave her anxious kisses with his enormous tongue. Airless kisses that hurt. She could see his face, eyelids shut tight, cheeks gaunt but taut. She could feel him rub against her, the hard zipper of his pants that he never wanted to take off. He showed her only his shin. Myelitis, Ella said to herself now, observing that foot in the past, wounded by the polio virus.

The Mother raised an eyebrow and murmured, that leg was the least of his problems, and then she considered the matter closed.

* * *

Be careful. Ella had asked to get sick so she could write, and though she did get sick she hasn't finished a single chapter. She's done nothing but jot down useless formulas and string together words *mistaken mangled blackened fireflies* on loose sheets of paper. She rubs her arm and tells herself, I won't get up till I finish, but she scans her screen and doesn't understand what she has done over these past months, what she was thinking about when she wrote down those scrambled phrases that now seem unconnected. Her idea has vanished. Her equation is confused. She gets up to smoke and sits down and gets up and gets back up and she fears she will never sit down again.

25

* * *

There's the doctor, standing by the door. Ella follows him, sits down to face images she can't decipher. What you can see inside the vertebrae is something more than the spinal cord. It's a raw irritation, a radiance two centimeters long. A spot. Mottled. Pallid. Transverse. And two lesions like nebulous lights in the darkness of the brain. What is not clear is the cause.

* * *

The diagnostic odyssey was beginning, but a diagnosis is nothing but a label on a body.

That label could say "viral condition in the spinal cord": some viruses are attracted to the nervous system, her Father confirms, not mentioning the guy with polio.

It could say "illness that attacks the tribes of another continent." *But you aren't black.* It's the Mother who ends that line by filling the screen with vehement exclamation points and question marks. *But we're all black, mom, you, me, your twins, my brother and my dad, and all the other inhabitants of this planet that's been stripped and melted and perforated by radiation.* Ella rereads her message before sending it and then she writes another. *Every time someone digs into their genes they always find black roots.*

Could it happen again? *¿Podría repetirse?* That's what Ella is afraid of, that while they poke around in her blood and find out what's causing that damage in her vertebrae, another piece of her nervous system will flare up. She directs the question by text to the Mother, because her Father answers only spoken questions. Could it happen again? This time Ella doesn't type the question, but dictates it, in her Mother's tongue, forgetting to change the keyboard from the language of the present. *¿Podría repetirse?* she dictates, and her phone transcribes: *For three out of 53.* She keeps going, amazed. Without raising her voice in a question she utters the phrase again, changing the intonation each time. *Podría repetirse. ¿Podría repetirse? ¡Podría repetirse!* And she contracts in astonishment reading what her phone translates each time. *Polity at it with you to see. Positive yet C. Polity up with you soon. But idiot up with you say.* And so on.

It could be a hereditary illness, a genetic predisposition. But her biological mother died too young to know and it's the other one, the one who doesn't share her genes, who suffered, like her, at the same age, from a problem in her spine. At thirty-five years old her leg just went to sleep. She was newly married when the doctors declared a deadly disease. She would have only a few months but they never told her, and the Mother, not knowing she was dying, decided to stop taking the medicines they'd prescribed. Not knowing she was dying, she got pregnant. She started to recover, unaware that her death was imminent. The Twins, she says, saved my life.

The Father collapsed with a bleeding ulcer when he found out that his second wife, destined to die as prematurely as the first, was pregnant with two. That doubled distress left him unconscious.

It could be a trap laid by a deteriorated defense system that can't recognize itself, that rejects itself by attacking its own organs, its tissues, its cells. That system could have inflamed her spinal cord, could be eating away at it to leave her paralyzed. Then Ella remembers she already has one of those autoimmune diseases. One that is corroding her thyroid. But that disease isn't serious, it's next to nothing, says the neurologist, raising his feathery eyebrows while his eyes scan a detailed lab report.

One by one the specialist rules out incurable and catastrophic diseases that might have been running through her veins. What he can't rule out through blood tests is that other malady, multiple sclerosis. Her brain shows two lesions and you need three to confirm sclerosis, says the doctor, while Ella carries out her own calculation: three spots, a single sclerosis that at the same time is multiple.

* * *

Ella already knew something about the sentence of sclerosis. Another summer, returning from another vacation, she noticed she'd lost a bit of shin. For that insensitive little piece she'd gone to the plastic-smiling neurologist, who had diagnosed her first pinched nerve. It must have been the only thing that doctor learned in his years at university, Ella thought now, as she listened to him say that it was better to have a compressed nerve than a progressive deterioration of the spinal cord. Now that's the kind of deadly disease you don't want to have, the specialist had said, sending her home with the thorn of sclerosis stuck in her spine.

And arteriosclerosis, what about that sentence? The redheaded neighbor Ella used to wave at over the fence of the past, who always said, when she left her keys in the refrigerator, when she didn't recognize her own yard or bought the same bouquet of carnations twice in one day, that she was having an attack of *la clora*. Ella had thought her solitary neighbor was feigning her forgetfulness to get attention, but now Ella herself is unable to find her keys and her glasses, to retain the number of planets in certain galaxies, or the faces and names of her students each semester, or even to recall her closest friends' last names. Sometimes she has trouble with her own name.

The neighbor had a mole under her eye that looked to Ella like an upset star.

Her red hair gone gray, still sporting the faded mole, the neighbor had been transferred to hospice. She had lost *house head hummingbirds*. Her own children were strangers she had come to fear.

* * *

Between sclerosis and arteriosclerosis was a deteriorated brain, endless ideas shipwrecked on the yellowish mass.

* * *

Sighting of a fist that rises up from the student body, a single dark hand and some fingers with polished nails that reach up to ask why the teacher referred so often to her head. My head? Several students nodded, yes, yes, your head and ours, everything's always about the head, says one, turn your head on, explode it, adds another, lose it, make it spin, and free it to imagine the universe. They had written her words down like a denunciation. Copperhead, blurted her only redheaded student. Empty-headed, the back row chorused, head-butting one another. Another accused Ella of having said she couldn't make heads or tails of her answer. Not to bury their heads in the sand. That two heads are better than one. The teacher had dared to tell them that no matter how many neurons they had in their heads they would always lack memory: an outdated smartphone was faster than any of their brains, but that didn't mean they had rocks in their heads. She didn't remember having said all that and she didn't understand why slowness seemed like an insult to them. That slowness made room for intuition and conjecture. It was like taking out your brain and placing it there, on a table, and letting the electric mass of its neurons illuminate you. She felt her head empty out while that morning's class waited for her to say something more, defend herself or feel regret, offer an apology. But the word head repeated so many times had made it incomprehensible. She let the full weight of her skull fall forward, those six kilos of bone, that kilo and a half of *proteins dew gray blubber* of a brain shot through with the likelihood of sclerosis. That was the neurological center of her insomnia: her head, not theirs, and not the heads in her words, but she wasn't going to tell them that.

* * *

The accusation hung over her head like an exposed wire.

* * *

On the street, at an antinuclear demonstration, walking beside El, who walks beside others carrying signs. Ella moves off toward the corner to make a long-distance call. There's too much shouting, horn blowing, slogans, barking dogs tearing at the air, her Father can't hear her well, and she goes into a café in search of silence. Her Father tries to calm her, assuring her she's not of sclerotic age. You don't have enough cerebral lesions. And the lesions of sclerosis are round, yours are long. And in any case, multiple sclerosis would be a *good* diagnosis. Good, she repeats, confounded and grim. Good? Talk louder, I can't hear you, Ella implores. Yes, good, can you hear me? answers the Father, his inaudible voice coiling through protesters. Or maybe he's gotten an elbow from the Mother, and that's why he clears his throat and then coughs. Well, *hija*, good compared with cancer.

Then it could be spinal cancer, Ella repeats in a daze when she hangs up and returns to the chaos of the street. That hadn't crossed her mind, but yes, it had. It had crossed before her eyes. She'd seen the word disguised in the MRI report: *Neoplasia or possible glioma cannot be ruled out.*

Repeat a hundred times: any word ending in oma is a malignant word.

Repeat that it could be cancer and that it would be terminal. The vertebrae are very narrow and the tumor's speed is inversely proportional to the patient's age.

It could be cancer. Could be. It could be, and it could be nothing. Idiopathic is the word that names that nothing, that never knowing: to be one among many patients left with no diagnosis. She would prefer that: if the problem lacked a name, she could ignore it. If there was no proof. Much as that not knowing was a form of knowing: to know what doesn't yet exist, to rest there.

It's nothing, says her Friend from the country of the past they shared, not until you know what it is. If a forensic scientist can't find a single bone fragment, he can't determine the existence of a body, its identity, its age. If an entomologist doesn't pin his insect, he can't study it. If the doctor doesn't receive samples, results, precise images. And she runs out of examples there. But both of them know that one doesn't always need to see to *believe think die suddenly*.

With the Mother's spinal issue, they never found out. After the double birth, her leg mended and the Mother stopped limping, she walked with firm steps, carrying the Boy Twin in one arm, and the Girl Twin, twice as big, in the other. More upright than ever, resuscitated by hormones, the Mother.

The Grandmother's case was different: a toe on her left foot went to sleep from overwork. She came back from the office honking the horn to announce her arrival, and she complained of an idiot or idiopathic toe that her doctor daughter mocked. One morning it was no longer the toe but the *foot thigh tongue tied*; hours later her mind was gone.

* * *

Intravenous steroids in explosive quantities followed by a slow descent on the roller coaster of pills: this is the recommendation from the laconic neurologist. Steroids to repair her short circuit.

* * *

Speech, whispered the futurologists, was a technology behind the times, slow and overly human. In the future there would be direct connections between brains and no one would need *compasses languages lies*. They forecast telepathy with broadband speed that Ella didn't need: she'd always had a telepathic relationship with her Father. She sends him a signal and the phone rings, carrying his voice to her.

Ella understands that her Father's hand is cupped around the mouthpiece as he asks if she needs money, if what he'd given her would cover the treatment, much as they both know that the Father can no longer come to her rescue. I could ask your brother, coughs the Father, or your mom, but Ella roundly refuses.

* * *

The Mother flies over the city of the present with its tall towers full of windows starting to light up. White. Green. Yellow. Her plane lands the same morning her daughter's atomic treatment begins.

The Mother plops down awkwardly in the waiting room while Ella is revived by the drug injected straight into her vein. And later on, that same Mother wakes up disoriented. Looks around. There are rows of green chairs and a fan haphazardly attached to the wall. An elderly lady pushes a metal walker, accompanied by a short old man who walks upright toward four secretaries dressed in blue. Then she presumes. On a side table, a stack of magazines under the portrait of the newly elected president. The titles in a language that isn't hers. Then she knows. She stands up and checks her purse, clutched under her arm; it's closed, everything inside, no one has stolen anything during her nap. She arranges her hair, poking fingers into the dyed-black thatch, checking that each lock is still in place, still attached to her skull. And she smooths her blouse with her hands, discreetly touches that numbed chest to be sure it's still in place, and makes sure that each button is in the right buttonhole.

The Mother walks with her arms bent outward, making room for a past corpulence. Her arms hollowed as if she were never going to recover from the kilos that once plagued her. She peers into the room where her daughter chews an insipid stick of gum and waits for the steroids to saturate her blood. There are so many sick people in there with her, hooked up to another slow poison. It makes the Mother remember the chemotherapy she survived more than a decade ago. She doesn't like to remember that, and plus there's nowhere to sit. The Mother shrugs her resigned shoulders to indicate she'll go back to the room reserved for those who wait. She takes a step or two in that direction and hesitates, stops, turns around, and warns her daughter that she's going to get fat. The Mother is gesticulating that phrase from the threshold. The daughter knits her brows in a question, trying to understand. And the Mother puffs up her cheeks and repeats what she'd said, expelling the air and raising her voice: don't worry, but be prepared. You're going to get fat. The daughter doesn't know if the Mother is condemning her or if getting fat would be a sign of improvement. Or if she's speaking from the hatred she still harbors toward her own corpulent past. Get fat, Ella thinks, watching the indecisive IV drip. What she wants is not to die.

Someone once said there are those who dare to express affection in illness. Or maybe it was that illness often takes on the disguise of love. The Mother has returned to the waiting room.

* * *

Everything suddenly goes up. Her blood pressure. Her adrenaline levels. Her lucidity. Her euphoria.

She does some figuring on a sheet of graph paper: she would need some months, maybe a full year, to come up with a new hypothesis and track down a professor who would bother to answer her messages. Someone else had already rebutted the theories of that old physicist, bushy-haired like her Father, and those of the theoretical physicist who, paralyzed in his mechanical chair, deciphered the world with a finger. She was postulating something narrower, more descriptive, something that could be undertaken in six or seven months. Maybe the milky way. Maybe just its hole, just one and not a grand theorem, something more finite, something small. There'd be no time to spare with seven months but I could do it, Ella thinks euphorically, spurred on by the second atomic dose that now thinks for her, dreams for her, and maybe if I hurried I could do it in less time, less, many fewer *years months dizzy spells sleepless nights*. Not so long to go! I'm almost there! Her pulse races and she understands that this optimism is chemical. Her confidence is made of steroids. To finish in a short time what she hasn't been able to do in years. And why do I want less time? she wonders then, exasperated, and she has no answer. Her ideas get scrambled and she feels an uncontrollable urge to vomit.

And it's at night when her worst thoughts arise, but she doesn't turn on the light, she doesn't want to wake up El, he's finally emerging from a season in hell after the explosion that almost killed him. If his sleep weren't so fragile and his mood so bitter these past months, she would get out of the bed they've shared for some years and go spend the night on the balcony where there's room only for her: she is soothed by the stars of her balcony, just knowing that they're invisibly there. She decides to lie still instead. Not to sigh. Not to cough. Not to clear her throat. To hold in the sneezes and the snores and let herself be rocked by the ticktock of the clocks in the kitchen. By the dripping faucet El doesn't know how to fix. The room closes in on her, every tick of the second hand illuminates the face of a guest at her funeral. The one Ella is planning for herself.

* * *

With the third shock of steroids her body temperature rises. I'm on fire, she sings, crazed; the nurse says mm-hmm and walks away. And once unplugged from the IV, she leaps from the chair and unleashes an outlandish peal of laughter and takes the stairs two at a time, followed, one by one, by the Mother. Automatic doors open and close. Her feet accelerate on the sidewalk and the Mother, atop heels, quickens her short, hard steps. Wait for me, the Mother implores, out of breath, but Ella can't wait. If she stops, the lid on her brains will slip off and her insides will be launched into the stratosphere, her wrapping of *skin polyester cotton*, her bare bones a heap on the pavement.

* * *

And the Mother insists that she rest but the drug won't let her and just like her Grandmother said, you sleep when you die. Her Grandmother, who would pull up to the house honking the horn three times so someone would come running out to open the gate. Her Grandmother, who claimed to dream as she sped through the streets. The Grandmother of the deadened toe who had already found her rest.

* * *

Not that Ella is cured. This is only a palliative treatment while they find a diagnosis and determine whether the medication has had a definitive effect. Meanwhile, she must not expose herself to all those people crammed into *restaurants cinemas stadiums classrooms subway cars bathrooms orgies*. All those people, so human and so animal, so covered in the worst kinds of fungus and bacillus against which she now has no protection. The neurologist hadn't warned her: In high doses, steroids destroy immune cells in order to stop the attack her body could be waging against her. Because sometimes the body has ideas of its own. Its revenge. Its assaults from behind.

The steroid is nothing but a momentary truce that leaves her body at the mercy of any passing infection.

The incompetent neurologist forgot to tell her, so the Father is the one who gives her the categorical order: immediately suspend her classes in the polluted city schools, lock herself inside four walls, and don't get close to anyone, not even El.

* * *

The downtime of her wait was perhaps the most elevated, the most alert, that steroid time making way through her veins, the time of the programmed destruction of her defensive system.

The immune system isn't based in any organ, the Mother says, interrupting herself to cover her mouth before coughing. It is, she says, a system in circulation, a moving brain that travels the body, always on alert. If it fails in its surveillance, the result is cancer;

if, on the contrary, it mistakes one's own cells for foreign ones and turns against them, it can kill you. In other words, says Ella, the cells that kill you are the same as the ones that cure you. In other words, says the Mother, correcting the daughter, if those cells don't defend against foreign bodies, or if they defend you even from your own cells, it means the system has gone bad.

404 error. System gone mad. Please restart.

* * *

If the Boy Twin caught a cold or flu, instead of isolating him, the Mother would put the Girl Twin in his crib and encourage them to kiss. Each other, their cousins, the daughters of her girlfriends and neighbors. The impure makes us healthy, the Mother declared in her authoritative voice. Exposing them to foreign bodies will make them stronger. And she decreed that if they threw food onto the floor they had to then put it in their mouths without washing it. Let no one stop them from eating *dirt rocks termite-infested sticks*. Rotten fruit. Potato peels from the garbage. The Lady, who didn't know how many years she'd been there standing or kneeling to work in that house, how many windows and floors she'd cleaned, how many dishes washed and dried, how many glasses broken on purpose, the children she'd bathed, the stews boiled, the jams stirred in pots, the secrets kept for some other day, that Lady who was the secret mistress of them all got upset with those orders, wincing. What kind of doctor was this filthy woman who wanted to get her children sick? And she soaked the fruit in bleach, scrubbed the vegetables with dish soap.

But the Twins never ever got sick, the Twins got fatter. What doesn't kill you makes you fat, the Mother said when she saw that her children, lying on the scale, had gained weight. The Girl Twin always weighed a little more.

And Ella wonders if the inverse of that saying could also be true. Because she, who has always been thin, still can't gain weight.

* * *

Though Ella has quit smoking, she accepts a cigarette from the Mother and they both smoke, and they both get a little dizzy, and together they remember how, when he still smoked, the Father used to send Ella to the kiosk to buy the packs he would consume that day. Walking strengthens the lungs and the heart, he'd say to persuade her, and you can keep the change. And she'd go down the sidewalk kicking pebbles and counting the lines between paving stones, until she put the packs of cigarettes in her pocket and a phosphorescent piece of gum in her mouth. She went back popping bubbles and counting the same lines in the sidewalk, the tinkling coins in her pocket now forgotten, because her real reward was to stop on the way to collect bits of concrete from the ground. To observe them in the palm of her hand. To wonder about the atomic composition of cement.

* * *

The Mother has set off back to the past, leaving the apartment full of nicotine and strands of her dyed hair stuck to the rug, threaded through Ella's underwear and El's. Ella goes around collecting those little pieces of Mother tangled in the corners, contorts her fingers in the drain to pull out that old-wire hair and separate it from her own, which is softer but accumulates there all the same. Ella deposits the Mother's hairs in a different jar; she's lived her life collecting, naming, labeling, and losing little pieces of dead material in containers of various sizes. She still has some *fingernails eyelashes gallstones paper stars*. And her Father's nails.

* * *

An old inventor had managed to bottle light, and Ella dreamed of bottling shooting stars.

* * *

The protest of undocumented migrants isn't long in coming. The avenues fill up with small flashlights and phone lights. Down with xenophobia! some of them clamor. Down with violence! cry the rest. El comes home early, covered in dust and with halos of dried sweat under his arms, and without changing, with no time to tell Ella about his day excavating new mass graves, he goes back out to join the chanting crowd. Don't wait up for me. That's El, haughty and stentorian, who slams the door and damages the hinge again.

From the second floor Ella sees him move off, surrounded by people who are strangers to her. El is her antiparticle, she thinks, her positron, the counterpart to the electron she has been. A positron that second by second is growing more distant.

She lights a cigarette in the open window, watching as the street full of people grows dark. The ember kindles each time she inhales, then subsides like a hydrogen-starved star. She lights another match and her fingers ignite. She lets out a curse full of confinement, talking to herself, alone with herself, her voice still livened by the drug. She starts to shout, this is our country too! joining in the slogans of the street as they pass in front of her, because though she can't go out, she is one of those people marching with posters and no papers, those people of every color and thickness and height. She is just a resident in the present of this country, she works in this city but isn't from here, not like El, who was born and raised and nearly died here a few months ago. She is just a temporary resident, an alien sick with who knows what. And she sits beside the window because now there are stars sewn to the night and protesters in the streets and police armed to the teeth, shielded to the eyebrows, ready to provoke an explosion, while El stays submerged in that crowd, wedged in, mixing with the crowd that today is also El.

Someone whistles and Ella shivers. Some young people blow frenziedly on giant horns and announce, we need each other, the world will end if we don't join together. She nods, circles her mouth with her hands, and hollows out her voice. The dream of purity is a nightmare! she shouts, already hoarse from so much smoking. Immunity will be our death! Someone stops in the street and looks for her voice, her rough, gravelly voice, and Ella yells louder, for the joy of yelling and for the urgent need to cry out in all directions, not caring whether that someone understands what she means when she howls, we are all infected, the infection is health, immigrants are life, immunity is death!

* * *

Until finally the steroid dissolves in her blood and Ella drops her backpack on the metal detector that checks for *knives axes ventriloquist weapons* entering the schools. Weapons no one will outlaw. Giving grades, bad grades, is riskier than hand-to-hand combat with illness, but now Ella prefers the danger of being there. Being there means not being dead, it means she is not dying. There. In that badly painted room, facing all those chairs filled with morning students who have little interest in whatever Ella can tell them about the uncertainty principle. She tries to be succinct: the universe has never known harmony, has never been a perfect mechanism, it's no good for measuring time precisely. She explains this while sitting on her long professor's desk, trying not to move too much, not to get worked up. She sees their bored faces from up close, sees how some of them turn half-closed eyes toward the clock on the wall. She follows the trajectory of their gazes and points toward the stopped hands that there's no budget to reactivate. Imperfect time, like the time of the universe, she repeats, but the bell interrupts her.

* * *

Apocalypse story. After the great planetary wars, atomic scientists tried to calculate how near the world was to its end. During several years of tense coexistence, the doomsday clock indicated that the world was three minutes from collapse. In recent years, that time had fallen to two minutes and thirty seconds. And even closer to the present, she tells other students, they'd been half a minute from uncertainty.

Those other students, the evening ones, observe her attentively: some with resentment, others, suspicion.

* * *

Though the temporality of space is a wave, Ella tries to draw a chronology of discoveries in a straight line on the blackboard. Frozen stars. White dwarfs and pulsars contracting and collapsing in millions of black holes scattered around the universe. And then the infinite density of the singularity and the event horizon from which it was impossible to return. The ephemeral suns of theoretical physics, and the emergence of nuclear physics during the planetary wars. Extraterrestrial physics. What happened next on that chalk line, though everything was occurring simultaneously. And Ella talks to the students and the minutes advance, though they seem to be moving backward or at least to have stopped, and then she feels a sudden spark in her fingertips.

Spontaneous electrical discharge in her hand. Instantaneous *ow* of pain twisting the thread of her words. The fraction of a second out of sync with her watch. She hides her hand in her pocket in case immobilizing it will prevent a second shock. Her students look up in surprise at her shrill cry, and they whisper as they try to figure out, among themselves, what's happening to their physics teacher now.

* * *

Portrait of a volt-charged hand that she can no longer extend to anyone.

* * *

As Ella hides her hand in her pocket, as she wraps her thumb in her fist, she again encounters her old biology professor. The difficult eyes of the teacher who didn't want to let her tag along on the visit to the morgue: Ella wasn't enrolled in the class. No, she wasn't, she agreed, but there was a reason she wasn't: she had learned the material over breakfasts and on the way to school and over meals and on vacations that were never restful, because that was when her Father and Mother dissected every case, going into pathological detail, shared symptoms, procedures. For her parents, everything started in the body and ended in illness, and what happened in between was part of that same endless conversation. But those are just words, she went on, I've never seen anything, and her voice was a complaint or perhaps an entreaty. Ella wanted to see the organs, smell them, maybe even touch them, and she didn't say lick them because that might worry the teacher. There will be no autopsy, the teacher said, cutting her off impatiently, but Ella caught the curiosity in her scowl and insisted she wanted to see the things she'd been imagining all her life. Though not just imagining, she admitted, unafraid of the truth. And the teacher cocked her head and narrowed her eyes, *suspicious indecisive green disgusted*, wanting to know more. I've seen some things. Where had she seen what? At home, Ella explained, on her Father's desk, in his illustrated books. And she started to recite not the organs—there were too many—but the systems in the body. Skeletal. Articular. Muscular. Circulatory. Lymphatic. Endocrine. Nervous. Immune. She'd learned them by heart, but what about the digestive system? That isn't really a system, it's an apparatus, Ella replied, squinting her eyes because a ray of sun had come from behind the ringed clouds to shine into the yard, into her face. Sunlight exploded on her eyelashes. The teacher further narrowed her eyes crisscrossed by neutrinos, and she was agreeing even as she shook her head, her whole figure tall and haughty, one hand stuffed into her pocket while the fingers of the other pushed her thick hair, dark and shiny, from her face.

Ella wasn't sure until she found herself aboard the school bus, and she sat in in the first seat, beside the biology teacher, who asked what her Father's specialty was. He didn't have one, but he was one of the best. Ella praised her Father because he was the only general practitioner she knew.

That preterit afternoon, on a bus crossing the militarized downtown of a city under ironclad dictatorship, the teacher said nothing more, and Ella was closer than ever to asking her about the hand she kept hidden in her pocket, that hand no one had ever seen, the hand that, everyone suspected, wasn't there.

* * *

Speculation about a sleeve sewn onto a pocket. In that hollow of cloth *useless nails rings missing or extra fingers.* The clipped end of her arm.

* * *

And Ella had taken her place around the dissection table that she remembers as wooden but that must have been aluminum, in a poorly lit room that was perhaps flooded with light. A cold and spicy scent *volatile flammable methylated* in her nose that she covered, even seeing that no one else did. Not the mute members of a scholarly sect who seemed to be worshipping those organs. A heart with severed arteries. A spleen swollen by leukemia. The double lung stained by the badly ventilated city air or perhaps the smoke of countless cigarettes. The wrinkled mass of the brain that the scalpel was about to cut in an anatomy lesson that Ella couldn't bear. Drunk on formaldehyde, mortified by disgust and retching, she had to flee, to breathe deeply and go back in, ordering herself to rise above the distress to witness the ceremonial opening of each organ. But all in vain, because she left again and entered again and then abandoned that improvised classroom forever.

She would never admit to her Father that she hadn't been able to look, that she'd had to run, that she chose to stick with the memory of the plastic organs adorning his desk. Those hard but hollow organs that, split open, were full of mystery.

* * *

El had told her that the bodies the morgue used were usually the ones that no one ever claimed. More migrant bodies made to disappear piece by piece.

* * *

Ella interrupts the whispering and talks to her students about the white mass found in her spine that sends her occasional *lashings electric eels*. As they do with other physical phenomena, the experts are evaluating theories, but haven't reached any conclusions. She doesn't want to complicate things, doesn't know if hers is a slow inner suicide. It's an inflammation of the vertebrae, she sums up out loud, seeing that some students are taking the opportunity to look at their phones, and others are calculating whether more classes will be canceled.

* * *

Their faces blurred as Ella called roll. She rubbed her eyelids, wondering what could be causing her clouded vision. She knew that another spinal attack could damage her optic nerve, and that conclusive proof would come in the color red. Her favorite color could also be the color of her illness. The signal: if red lost its intensity in one of her eyes. She had to close them alternately, compare and report—to herself, in the absence of a specialist—on whether she noticed any difference between one red and another.

You don't see well because you don't clean your glasses, El fumed, exhausted by the constant consultation of symptoms. El, who would rather die of the flu than admit he had it. El, who took painkillers only under threat of death. Who never went to the doctor. Who preferred not even to consult Ella. Who cleaned his glasses conscientiously when he woke up, who examined cracked bones with impeccable corrective lenses. Her own glasses were always covered in fingerprints. And El tried to take her glasses from her, to clean them.

The touch of his hand full of static, and, between them, a strange flickering.

* * *

An ancient philosopher had been convinced that light came from the eyes, that eyes emitted light; otherwise, he said, the most distant stars would not be visible. This philosopher had concluded that the speed of ocular light must be absolute.

Explaining the speed of light, Ella tells the students in another class that a missile would be capable of crossing millions of kilometers in a thousand seconds to fall right onto the school entrance. Less than eighteen minutes, sparks one student, alarmed by how little time they would have to find a refuge that doesn't exist. But the missile's speed is not the speed of light, which anyway isn't the fastest anymore, Ella replies, adding that the layers of electromagnetic refraction in the atmosphere present a lot of resistance. Real speed is the speed of light in a vacuum, she says, but that doesn't console her student.

* * *

Ella doesn't notice any improvement, but neither is she any worse. This doesn't console her either.

* * *

Who will be her attending physician in the future? Her unattending physician announces that what she has is not sclerosis, flashes his false smile at her for the last time, and hands her off to a female and less fleeting colleague, taller and much less idiotic.

At her first appointment, Ella scrutinizes the neurologist whose translucent eyes enlarge when they review her file on the screen. A fixed, dry gaze that hasn't learned how to blink. This neurologist is missing something, she still doesn't know what. Ella lets her talk about the strange things that other, older doctors can't understand, more versed as they are in the rigid labels whose checklist of symptoms her body is resisting. The neurologist smiles, seems to be enjoying her broad repertoire of knowledge, *axon sheaths signs foraminal stenosis*, and more words offered with a voice that's soft but not sweet, a voice that doesn't hesitate. Myelin. Myelitis. Myelopathy. Now unsmiling, she repeats each term as though afraid

Ella hasn't understood the language of cryptic concepts, though the patient has in fact already studied them. Ella focuses her attention on the slight lines around the neurologist's mouth, on her thin, unlipsticked lips, on her brown hair with black roots, on her still hands on the keyboard, and she goes on examining her until she realizes what is missing. The stethoscope. The kind that hangs from the Mother's neck like a languid tie and peeks from the Father's pocket, a rubber earthworm with an aluminum head that slides coldly along her memory, down her back, over her flat chest, checking that inside her there's a hollow organ, sonorous as a drum, surrounded by the silent cavity of her lungs. But the neurologist doesn't have a stethoscope, not around her neck or tucked away. How long has it been, Ella thinks as she watches her doctor, since anyone listened to her heart?

Only El places his ear over her chest, every once in a while.

* * *

Take revenge on that vocabulary with another that her neurologist doesn't know, lob her a *wavelet accretion g(z) g(-z)* in the universal language of mathematics that, like any language, is understood only by those who use it. *Fullerenes fermions convolution.* Muons heavier than electrons. Toss out pieces of that language Ella speaks only with herself.

* * *

Would this neurologist be the one to cure her?

And who was the woman who strolled the stony streets of Ella's childhood? She came up to their beach house and knocked at its door, all signs of her humanity gone. Her *lips pupils pencil-drawn eyebrows.* Her head wrapped in a rag that aspired to be a turban.

47

And with a wave of her hands the Mother makes the daughter disappear as her mouth draws the word cancer that this woman wore like a crown.

There was another woman, but Ella never knew who it was. The Father had stopped at the hospital to pick up some documents, and he brought her with him through *stairways rooms mops shadows*, through consulting rooms opened and shut. They'd taken a shortcut on the way out, turning down a hallway that took them through the x-ray department. There the Father stopped, absorbed in the screen where they both saw a series of slices of a brain cut in two. A brain like an open book. The exposed matter of thoughts. As he leaned over the screen, the Father's long finger traced the perimeter of the skull and the curves of the wrinkled interior, and he stopped on a white spot. Look, he said, see this? The cerebral mass got smaller in each cut, while the spot got larger, encrusted into the bone. A ball, compact like a punch. That must hurt, Ella said, without understanding what she was seeing.

* * *

But why do you think you have cancer?

Her memory revives her maternal grandfather's throat cancer and her uncle's meteoric colon cancer. The metastatic pancreas and liver cancers of her aunts. The breast cancer they removed from the Mother.

None of them hereditary, but all bad omens.

And her gym teacher coworker had grown so thin that when Ella went to visit her she walked right past her in the common room. She heard someone calling her from behind, from afar, from a now ancient era that still vibrated with her name. She turned to look at her but found only drawn lips, a pair of prominent cheek-bones. Jumpy, yellowed eyes. A pile of bones hydrated through an IV.

And she had almost forgotten the cellist's father. Did the Mother remember? Her acquaintance's father was a well-known orchestral musician. His head hurt, his fingers went numb as they played the piano. The doctor insisted the man was suffering from too much touring, too many concerts, too much sleeping in foreign beds in a different city every night. The changes in altitude and all that alcohol weren't good for him, suggested the doctor, even though the cellist's father had stopped drinking.

Only after ruling out all the physical causes could you suggest a psychological cause, said the Father. Or exhaustion. Or the stress that explains everything by explaining nothing. Physical causes, repeats Ella, the physics expert without a degree.

* * *

Forget about cancer, her Father said, immediately sorry he'd used that word again. I mean, he said, forget about *that*. She had to re-mind him that the radiologist still hadn't ruled out a tumor and the neurologist had asked for a sample of cerebrospinal fluid. Ella had assumed they were still looking for the proteins of sclerosis or something stranger, but when she asked, already naked, already sitting on the cot and hunched over, the intern read the order and had to admit they were looking for cancerous cells.

* * *

The intern had explained to her that it would be like the needle of an epidural. Have you had kids? No, Ella said, feeling a stabbing in her spine.

The intern had said: This shouldn't take more than five minutes. Fifteen at most. You're thin, that helps a lot. But over half an hour has passed and the intern has already inserted five thick needles between three vertebrae, which have given Ella four electric shocks from her thigh to the tips of her toes.

How much does it hurt? It was the intern behind her asking Ella to measure her pain. Why was it that doctors and their assistants asked for pain in numbers from 1 to 10? Could it be said that 1 was pain? And what was 10? What could it be measured in relation to? To how much one could endure before losing consciousness? To the worst pain she could remember? But all the pain stored in her memory disintegrated under those needles that made her bellow a 6, an uncertain 8.

Any pain in the present is always the worst pain imaginable.

* * *

Once Ella ventured a 5 while the doctor wrote 9 in her clinical history. He was convinced that women subtracted pain from their pain. The next time she went with a 9. The nurse looked at her with a cross eye, affirming in a volcanic voice: at 9 you would be howling.

And maybe a threshold existed, a maximum intensity that the nerves refused to register. Maybe 10, the unsayable number, meant fainting. Preventive closure. Her Father faltered in the face of pain. Ella had seen him fall unconscious down a deep corridor, unable to stand the shock his body was giving him.

* * *

Her Father had taught her to count so that everything would have a number.

Do you often have back pain? It's the intern, who is still behind her trying to find her spinal fluid. No, never, the patient grunts impatiently, lying on her side, curled up on the cot. Except in the classroom, she adds, thinking that her lower-back pain in the classroom can't compare with what the intern is doing to her. The puncture. The shriek that escapes her as she's electrocuted by her own nerves.

From 1 to 10 is the question, 13 the reply. And if they manage to extract that transparent liquid, she'll need bed rest to stop the pain in the gummy mass of her brain stripped of water, sodium, potassium, and rare phosphates, of *calcium chloride amnesiac moths* that surround it and protect it.

* * *

No, not a medical doctor, Ella replies, and she can't avoid another blink of pain in her voice. I'm a physicist. I teach physics. But she knows her knowledge gives her away. The doctor inside her has been discovered by a fellow in the trade.

The question came from way back. That repeated grumble. Undergraduate degree in physics? Doctorate in what, dead stars? Work with the living, murmured the Father. But they were alive, those stars that sometimes moved in unexpected ways, tugged at by the gravity of some nearby galaxy. Even dead, those stars continued emitting their preterit gleam.

* * *

Dammit, sighs the intern when Ella suggests they give up on the puncture. The needle should be in the spine but it's going into something else. You must have an anatomical variation, let me try one more time? And she goes on practicing between the vertebrae of Ella's variation.

She's been told this before: She's the crooked one. Weird. *Out-of-place strange bird.* She blurts out nonsense too often. Gets tangled up between two languages, the one she writes and the one she speaks. She forgets certain words as if she lived with a constant neuronal short circuit. She says to herself, agitated with hatred, and she says to El, that her vertebrae are crooked or that's what they've told her, and she'll have to repeat the exam under a screen. So the inexpert entomologist can finally stick a pin through her back.

* * *

Her Father has never been as emphatic as he is on this call: The lumbar puncture should not be repeated. Why do they want to dig around in there, drain it, and vacuum—what?—when nothing can be done now, they would have had to do it before the steroids. Any manipulation has its risks, and the spine is delicate. Bunch of incompetents, declares her Father, hissing in her ear. And Ella pauses before reminding him that they're still looking for cancer. She's whispering that cancer, she's covering her mouth with the phone because she's surrounded by students taking a test in silence. It's not cancer, huffs the Father. Get that cancer out of your head, you know the diameter of vertebrae? If it were cancer you'd already be dead.

* * *

And when she hangs up the phone her hands are itching the way they've itched every time she thinks about the fact that her Father will die. Itching, it was her Father who told her, is pain's little sister.

We have to rule out the presence of malignant cells, insists the cautious neurologist as Ella rubs her hands on her pants. Wouldn't she be worse off if she had cancer? Wouldn't she already be underground? Ella practices a paternal tone as she questions the doctor, who replies in a murderous voice that some types of tumors recede temporarily with steroids, and that could be Ella's case.

And that reply pulverizes her, but she rises from the ashes determined to betray her Father. Betray him again, over the possibility of a tumor, over a doctor who knows about nothing but spines, and maybe not so much about those, Ella thinks, her hands balled in fists, her palms sweaty. The itching grows more intense.

The first betrayal was to reject medicine for a science that explained it all, the microscopic and the macroscopic. The second betrayal was to waste the Father's retirement and lie about it to his face. Her final betrayal would be to spurn his advice.

* * *

At the hospital they'd assured her they would set up an appointment for that puncture under a precise screen, but the days go by and no one calls. She checks her phone. Her calendar. Every Tuesday is one week less.

A Tuesday is another Tuesday is another Tuesday.

Her eyeglasses languishing on her desk.

Ella finds the number for the neurological institute and asks to speak with her doctor. The secretary demands a reason to interrupt. The possibility of cancer strikes Ella as more than enough reason, but she doesn't say tumor, doesn't say *carcinoma growth sanguinary cells*, she doesn't know why she subtracts malignity from her words. But she does know. She knows that the patient's anxiety makes others lose their patience. She knows that the disobedient are stigmatized, those who doubt, who question, who oppose—the naysayer patients. No one wants to deal with other people's desperation. The immutable secretary sounds distracted, or maybe she's shopping for underwear on her screen while she repeats that the doctor is busy. The hospital will call her, that old labyrinth of lime and steel rocked by tremors of the earth, that building full of elevators that swallow people up. They'll call her when the hospital finds it convenient to do so. But who is the hospital? Ella wonders, as the secretary informs her that she isn't the only sick person and the waiting lists are long. She is no one. No one. She already knows that. She's no more than the electrochemical bric-a-brac of millions of cells as nervous as those of anyone with a terminal outlook. And the secretary lets her know that she's taking a look at her file and sees that Ella will have to repeat the blood tests. Her previous sample is about to expire. Her cells explode, take aim at her, at Ella, who already paid for that blood, for the needle and the five tubes labeled with her name. She demands an explanation, knowing it's the wrong demand, that the mere word sends her into the corner with the difficult patients that the neurological institute is unwilling to accept. The intermediate secretary hands the receiver to the head secretary, who, *odious upset synapses* by that interruption of her routine, repeats the script the other had already recited.

To be nothing but synapse was to be animal.

* * *

And she hasn't needed to betray her Father. Another Thursday passes, another Tuesday, another Friday that finds her calling from hell again to make demands of the hospital.

* * *

Rewinding a decade in time toward her cancer, the Mother, back on the phone now: I don't have any bad presentiment about this. I never told you but I had some horrible months before finding my tumor. Ella imagines the Mother with *palpitations nightmares birds on the wire*, while the Mother continues, I didn't know where those nervous symptoms came from or who they were about. I didn't know they were about me. The Mother says this but falls short of the truth: she's always had those palpitations, and in her frequent nightmares she's gradually killed them all off. The strange thing is for her to now be saving Ella.

The Mother has mostly killed off the Father, who should be the first to go according to the law of sequential time, but she's also altered the order and dreamed of the Twins' death. She's left them unattended in a bathtub full of water or locked in the car under a scorching sun, forgetting them when she went to work. She's seen their two bodies in a single coffin, a head at each end, touching each other's mouths with their feet.

* * *

If the Twins were late coming back from school, it was Ella's mission to call the hospitals and make sure they weren't there. Stuck to the refrigerator was a list the Mother made with the numbers of all the hospitals, clinics, and the morgue. And the Twins had fun with it, testing the Mother with their delays. And they also put their sister to the test. Those Twins who, though not such siblings of hers, were her responsibility: the Mother called from her office to find out whether they had come back yet, and Ella said they had, even if it wasn't true.

* * *

Electronic, El calls to Ella from the doorway—or Electrocution, Element, or Electricity, but most often Electron—the keys still hanging from his hand. Where are you? I don't see you. My charge is low, she replies from a sofa strewn with papers, where it's already night. All that research. Everything she wrote with her sleeping arm is illegible, wasted time. Everything that came after, the long parentheses. Now I'm never going to finish, she says, letting him hear abdication in her voice, and then, hiding her resignation, she talks with nostalgia and relief about the massive suns that die condensed in a singular point of infinite gravitational force, that rend nearby stars and devour their light. Those stars fleeing from her eyes, sinking into cosmic gutters where everything disappears. But the holes scatter small particles of matter, he replies, citing Ella, because she's the one he learned it from. The holes aren't completely black.

Ella reproaches herself, thinking how her Father lives in the depths of her black hole.

* * *

Time doesn't count but it passes, the day comes. Ella crosses the doorway into the magnetic field, again, and again lies down on the resonance bed that slides into the tube. And she closes her eyes so its rays perforate her without touching her, and she opens them, and again she wonders how they manage to keep the ceiling of the room impeccable while everything else is falling to pieces, and she rises from her body and dresses it and returns to her house and sleeps and dreams fitfully and wakes up as exhausted as when she lay down, showers indifferently, but under the water collects *words phrases fossils from other eras* and she goes clumsily out into the street, gets onto dirty metro cars that cross the city swift as days, senseless, directionless, car after car, day after day, after day.

And the one who calls her now is the neurology assistant, to inform her that the spinal inflammation has gone down. The assistant's expectant breathing fills the void that Ella hollows out with her silence. Isn't that good news? The question sounds like a plea.

And she doesn't understand why she keeps going over that conversation in her mother tongue, when it occurred in another.

* * *

At the other end of the line the Father recites his diagnostic questions. The burning is gone. Yes. The tingling, yes. The numbness. She would rather not contradict him, but, though the reply is always yes, her hand is still suffering *shocks sparks painful wasps* in her fingertips. If she showers with hot water. If she washes the dishes. If she puts lotion on her feet, always rough. If she talks too much or bursts out laughing, if she waves her hands in retreat, if she writes on the board and covers her lips with chalk. If she inclines her head. If she drops it to her chest: another shock wave of electricity.

Your wires are stripped, kiddo, that's all, declares the Father. They'll go on sending you signals until they heal.

Her nervous system kept the memory *failed twisted useless* of an injury and went on reliving it—that was one explanation. But if my nervous system has a memory, Ella thinks, too slow—thinking in the present and maybe also in other times—if my body can remember, then it must also be able to forget.

explosion

* months earlier *

On leave for a few days. Forbidden to get up or engage with anything that might upset him. Ella had reminded him the night before but El ventured to open the door a crack, to bend over and reach out with his arm: his hand clenching the rolled-up newspaper bound with a rubber band. The newspaper he shouldn't read during these days of recovery. The newspaper he would hide from Ella.

El closed the door gently so as not to wake Ella, and he stood still for a moment, waiting. Stock-still. Feeling like something had been trapped in the air, out there, somewhere in the building. A whisper. An echo that had to be an auditory hallucination. His anvil and stirrup pounding senselessly in one of his ears. He knew that those crackling sounds existed only inside him. He couldn't trust his eardrum yet, but he sensed that now he was hearing a sound that came from outside his body. The neighbors' rustling Sunday. Ella's snores. The coffee maker burbling in the kitchen. It wasn't any of that, wasn't the rain, the coffee, an obstructed nose. It was a *vibrating living vital* sound. And again El's face peered out, marked by burns, his ear bandaged, and again he heard a trembling *e* in the hallway, a long *eeeee* that ended in consonants. A covert, continuous *heeeeelp*. A voice crying out?

Ella would berate him later for having crossed the threshold in a t-shirt and undershorts, for having gone in search of a possibly imagined voice heard through *walls ears uneven scabs*. For going down the stairs alone when he was on bed rest, and round-trip along another corridor, and then back up again to the apartment where that drawn-out word seemed to originate.

* * *

Description of an ashy head defeated by old age. It barely moves at the sound of running steps approaching.

* * *

This is an old-folks' home, Ella said bitterly when El woke her up to tell her about the collapsed old man bleeding from his nose. About the arm stretched out over the tiles, still holding the newspaper like a torch. Who knows how long he'd been there, laid out in the drafty hallway? El said, trying to keep her from judging him for going out alone in that state. Good thing you saved him, Ella murmured with a grimace, narrowing her eyes, oozing indignation.

But El deflected her silent reproach, still disturbed by the image of the old man he'd rescued from the floor and lowered into a chair and served a glass of water. He couldn't forget how when he'd offered to call an ambulance, the old man had adamantly refused. Please leave, the man had begged. And El had left the old man inside.

El hadn't even thought to ask his name, or hadn't dared. The nameless could always disappear.

* * *

A muscle or a tensed nerve, a twitch between the eye and the cheek was what Ella saw in El's face when his boss asked him to cut his leave short, to return and take over the on-site investigation, well aware that he shouldn't get close to an excavation site that had sent him headfirst into the hospital and all the others to the cemetery. The psychiatrist had prescribed distance from that mass grave and all others, for a time. But the director couldn't do the job and El was her number two.

I have to be away for a few days on strictly personal matters. That's how the director's memo to the team began. Only with El had she set euphemisms aside to confide how just that morning, she'd awakened to find her husband staring at her with imploring eyes, open too wide. Neither asleep nor awake.

Are you going to take over? Ella asked him, raising her voice. What would you do? El asked, shrugging his shoulders and slamming the door, again.

* * *

They realized the old man from the fifth floor had died when they saw, posted in the building's entryway, the for-sale notice. The real estate agent opened the door for them with veiny hands; the skin sagged around her neckline but not on her newly stretched face, which shone with lotion and fair loan prices. She wanted to hide what they already knew, but she confessed, with a note of resignation, that some people went to hospices to wait *sitting fallen fainted panting* for their turn to come, and others preferred to end their lives attended by strangers in hospitals. But not that old man, who'd decided to die alone in his own apartment. To that end, he'd bought the forty-five square meters the agent was now showing them. The same woman with starched and wrinkled skin had sold it to the deceased man just a few months before, and she could offer them a discount. Would they by chance be interested?

* * *

El dreamed he opened the old man up, using both hands to tear his hide like a rag, before cracking open his breastbone and finding himself inside, singed. Other times he found only *brushes needles traction devices* inside the old man. A telephone full of copper. An ear. A bloody scalpel. Sometimes the old man was wearing the same uniform as the dead workers. Sometimes El was one of the workers himself, or his bones were among those found in the mass grave before the explosion splintered them.

Sometimes El howled in his sleep, or muttered words in a language Ella could not decipher. She shook him. He woke up sweating with a sharp pain in his chest, sure he was having a heart attack.

The heart was a muscle that could give out.

El accused Ella of having filled his head with surgical nightmares. You and your family, body addicts, she heard him say as he threw off the sheets and punched the wall so hard it shook her. As if you didn't work with worse bodies, *muzzled broken dissolved in acid explodable*. She didn't need to remind him about the mined cadavers of the most recent dig. The splinters of those bones encrusted in his face, his ear cut, eardrum busted, face spattered with the blood of the workers who'd acted as a shield. It's a miracle you're alive, Ella raged. Ella, who dedicated her life to inoffensive dead stars.

He had always been irascible, but the explosion had made him even more bitter.

The Father issued contemptuous judgments of this profession that didn't diagnose or cure or make any attempt to do so. He was of the opinion that this man of forensics intervened only once it was too late, and even then it was just to establish dates of death using carbon 14. Instead of calling him by his name, her Father asked about that man or the historian, the bone guy. Only when El was taken to the emergency room did he become worthy of paternal respect. The Father asked about each of El's contusions and was surprised there wasn't a single broken bone; he was likely thinking how that same accident would have pulverized his Firstborn.

Ella, who had admired the luminous projection of El's skeleton in the hospital, could confirm that he was excessively radiated but in one piece.

El's only sister had been dying, like everyone, since childhood, and she went on having birthdays, as so many do, every April.

She called him every day while he was home on leave. His single sister's name flashing on the screen, the ringing phone piercing the silence, but since El rarely heard it, Ella was the one who answered. Then El would bellow a greeting designed to travel across the wide country that separated them. He spoke so loudly Ella could hear the expanding waves of the conversation even with the door closed.

How could they ever understand each other, Ella wondered, when instead of alternating sentences, their words overlapped and the decibel level climbed?

I'm going to go deaf, Ella scolded him, her open computer under her arm.

Bad idea to mention deafness. He was the one who'd lost his hearing.

* * *

The radiator building up steam and hissing softly in the living room, and the distant whistle of the trains crossing the nocturnal horizon of the present. And the ambulances, the honking horns, the thrum of nearby motors. El woke up knowing exactly what time it was, and if he was wrong it was only by a few minutes.

He slept so little. You can't go on like this, Ella said. She, ever since she was little, would lie down on the balcony to count stars when she couldn't fall asleep. Take something, she told El.

He didn't take anything, because even that decision required effort.

* * *

Are you going to take over that dig? Ella asked. You'd do it, too, El said, picking at a scab until he pulled it off, depositing it in her outstretched hand.

* * *

The explosion is still inside his eardrum.

Inside, El still has those workers fallen with their chisels, picks, scrapers, dustpans, stopped watches on their wrists. He's seeing them crouched down in the pit where there is only dust, rocks, torn bee wings, bits of flesh scattered in the smoke: an airborne bonfire. And fleeting sparks falling onto him, burning his hair, spattering his skin, wounding his clothes. An infernal sound and urine and blood mixing with dirt. People are running so fast around him and the fog is wafting so slowly, in such silence, that El thinks he is dead or paralyzed or abandoned to his fate and he closes his eyes, until he smells an acrid sweat and deduces that he's being carried out among several people who load him into a taxi that will whisk him away.

The taxi driver keeps an eye on him in the rearview mirror and talks to him so he won't fall asleep: that's the mission he's been handed, for which he's been paid triple what it would cost to bring an uninjured man to the hospital. Unaware that El can't hear him, the taxi driver decides to keep his attention by telling him about a time he made a distracted mistake that could have been fatal. I gave myself my insulin injection twice, because, listen here, don't fall asleep on me, because this gets good, I gave myself an overdose that made me crazy, an electroshock of current in my head, and it was only by some miracle I didn't die, listen here, he's shouting now, and it's a good thing I wasn't driving, listen, listen, and he stops at a light and shakes his passenger with one hand because now El's eyes are closing.

* * *

The nurses who pulled him from the taxi gesticulated with *fingers elbows flapping jaws*, talked to him with delayed voices.

The strange voice that was Ella's when she arrived in a flash at the hospital.

* * *

65

Lit up by the otoscope, the perforated eardrum was a planet wounded by an asteroid.

* * *

Futurist portrait in the intensive care unit. El was alert, aware, conscious but dazed. The explosion could have killed him but he's alive, alive, dozing, his closed eyelids move in slow motion, or maybe those are his eyes moving like worms beneath them. Ella wants to press a single kiss on his eyebrow, because El's face is all burns and winding bandages. A two-dimensional face. Her mouth hovers over the tip of a rough nose but there are many noses now. El is five bodies, eight ages, six swollen eyes, fifteen pairs of torn lips.

Ella tries to say something to pull him from the comatose buzz of his breathing. His eyes blink so slowly, so deliberately, as if they hurt. Positron, she calls him, whispering. Posi, she repeats, raising her voice. Positron, are you there? Give me a sign. She sees a tongue peek through the wound that is his mouth, she wets a finger with saliva and puts it to his lips so he'll know she is there. And she comes closer and tells him anxiously that the pit exploded, that all the others are dead.

He was trying to decipher what she said but there was noise in his head, and of all Ella's words he could discern only the end, because she switched to his language to say the phrase big bang.

* * *

Ella goes back to their shared apartment without the living nearness of his body. The empty living room. Empty chairs. The barren refrigerator. Dirty dishes. The unmade bed. She flops onto the sheets and dials the number of the past so she can tell her Father, consult him. Dad? she says almost without saying it, dad, dad, because she can't manage anything but incomplete words that disappear into her Father's ear.

* * *

Words falling off the cliff of his ear: the doctor didn't warn him, or maybe he did, but El didn't know that he might hear a whistling sound when his hearing began to come back. The daily noise would muffle that constant sonorous thread, but it would seem louder in the stillness of the night. The sound filled him with insomnia.

And there were people who lost their minds with that sound embedded in their heads. People who killed themselves just to get silence back.

* * *

Now Ella was turning that ring on her finger that didn't signify any kind of commitment. Turning over that conference where she'd seen him in profile and head-on and had imagined him *graying wrinkled curled over a cane.* She'd wanted to shrivel with him. To gradually wear out every one of her vertebrae with him. To have felt that now leaves a hole in her stomach.

* * *

They're running through an airport so they won't miss the connection that will take them to the country of the past where they met. She'd been a student on vacation in her city, he was a forensic scientist invited to give a master class on identification of the bones that abound in the earth of countries like hers, disturbed by years of dictatorship. Ella's Friend, who went to all those talks as if it were her duty or her form of mourning, had invited her to the conference in the newly inaugurated museum of memory, where El, with hair still very thick and black, all his teeth, arrogance in his smile and a badly tied tie, spoke of the time trapped in carbon 14, and how every bonologist should leave the laboratory and get his or her hands dirty on a dig. He moved his own hands as he spoke, and there was no ring on his finger.

That country of the past was sown with still-undiscovered graves.

The city of the present was now finding its own. Hundreds of clandestine graveyards full of anonymous cadavers, though everyone knew who they were.

Migrants crossing borders or trying to, abandoned along the way, dying frozen or gagged or suffocated inside trucks, wrapped in newspapers whose pages confirmed their date of death, women hacked to pieces and children lost in arid lands that halted their disintegration and the passage of time. El had exhumed those cadavers on the outskirts of the present.

El had gone into bone identification in order to put an end to violence. That's what he told her when they met. Ella found the effort heroic.

* * *

Now Ella is bringing El back to the past, this time without a tie, to introduce him to her family. She tugs on his arm, hurries him along, we're going to miss our connection, but El falls behind, and when Ella turns to be sure he's following her, he has disappeared. The plane is ready to take off, the last stewardess is about to board, they're the only ones left. And that woman dressed in red, a little red hat and red heels clicking on the floor, is raising her hand to wave at Ella. Ella doesn't know what to say, how to excuse El's delay. There is no one but her on the terminal's white tile floor, until finally a pallid El appears. I don't feel so good, I'm a little queasy, he stammers, after emerging from the bathroom he's been locked inside for the past seven minutes. Ella howls at him, they're going to leave us behind. And El drags his moccasins and his heavy legs and holds out his blue passport and disappears down the walkway, followed by the annoyed stewardess. No sooner do they sit down and buckle their seat belts than she realizes that El is racked by fever and cold. She throws her blanket over him, hers and that of the passenger beside her, plus two or three more brought by another red-clad stewardess. The hours and the years stretch out as if instead of heading toward the past, they were all on their way to Mars. And if El is still trembling it's not because the six blankets aren't working but because he is dehydrated. He can't take even a sip of water without it coming back up. He regurgitates everything he's eaten that day, but he's trying to stifle the retching noise that aggravates the nearby passengers, who have already started to eat.

Just a little gastric unrest, he murmurs, disturbed by the vomiting.

Her Father would think of *dengue yellow fever malaria chikungunya*, or he'd think of something much worse. Ella doesn't know what to think.

* * *

El was convinced that the cold weather brought on stomach cramps and he blamed the city's winter, its endless snows, the slippery ice camouflaged on the sidewalks. Ella knew the cold didn't cause his indigestion, just as it didn't cause colds or urinary tract infections.

He'd always had a problem with onions, and he stopped eating them, just like he'd quit *chili pepper cauliflower fungus*. And beans. Sardines. Cucumbers. Some packaged cookies sent him running to the bathroom and he had to stop buying them. But during those long days down in the mass graves, he ate whatever poison they put in front of him. God forbid he be labeled snooty by the excavation workers, who devoured salami and raw onion on bread and smacked their lips. Ella loved the garlic that made El ill.

Sick all the time. Swollen belly, all the time. As he vomited on the plane one might have said his stomach hurt right down to the pylorus. Her girlfriends used to say that in school and double over laughing; Ella would smile, wondering if they knew, those classmates of hers, where that pain was really to be found.

* * *

El started to follow the dog's diet: nothing, until he was better. But her Father had tried that diet, and the acid had eaten him away inside until he was hollow. There was no way to convince El that his thinness was growing dangerous. He said he'd lost his appetite. She ate for both of them, fighting her own disappearance.

To lose kilos of *fat muscle nerves caffeine*, to lose the desire to get out of bed. To lose his laughter, the echo of his former cheer. To lose the desire to be with Ella, to laugh with her, ever since he almost lost his life in that fiery mass grave.

* * *

He'll have to stay on investigating that pit, which has become an unprecedented political scandal. Until his boss comes back. At his office, El sends her a text he's just dictated into his old phone. *She's not going to come back so soon, now she says she's going to spend 34 days at a conference.* Ella reads it in consternation and writes, *What do you mean 34?! What kind of conference lasts 34 days?!* but right away another text comes from El, *no comma I said 3 to 4 excla-*

mation point it's 4 days comma the go down shoe. And another one comes immediately: *my goddamn shrew of a boss period this phone is deaf exclamation point it doesn't know how to interpret what I say exclamation point exclamation joint.*

That excavation should not be your responsibility, Ella insisted, not that pit or those dead people, even if your boss isn't there. El raises a pair of anguished eyes and places a finger over his lips while he looks around the room. The walls could have ears.

* * *

Traces of stitches scoring his face. Marks from scabs he's picked off his forehead, leaving scars. El is down to skin and bones. But he hasn't lost the tan from the blazing sun that beat down on him and through everything, *helmet uniform sunscreen*, his anthropologist's short gray hairs. But his eyes are sunken from the attempt to find out who had conspired in that massacre, which repeated in his own city what was also happening in others. Who had blocked the investigation and murdered part of his team? Who had untrained the bees used to detect explosives on-site? El wondered, unhungry.

El had led that operation. El had believed he'd implemented an efficient tracking technique, as discreet as a buzz, because bees were easier to transport than dogs and cleaner than rats and had equally refined senses of smell. They didn't have noses but they did have antennae that responded to minuscule molecules, subtle vibrations, variations in temperature and changing degrees of humidity. They recognized one another because they carried the smell of the hives they inhabited.

Bees were able to detect a micron of pollen and pick it up with their hairy feet charged with static, and they could locate other particles present in the air. They'd been trained like dogs or rats: made to associate the smell of explosives with that of sugar water. Instead of salivating, they extended their crops as if to extract nectar from a flower. But the area of that mass grave was too big, and it was surrounded by gardens that perhaps distracted them. That had been their mistake.

* * *

A 404 error indicated that the search term could not be found or didn't exist. The bees were lost or unavailable, but to exist and not be accessible was a 410 error.

* * *

The tension was simmering. El was getting threats, anonymous ones slipped under the door. More than his hearing hung in the balance, but he couldn't say that to Ella, and so he stopped speaking to her.

Speech was in the left hemisphere of the brain, but the right one wasn't mute; it had something to say about fear.

The stomach filled with acid, its way of expressing itself.

* * *

Go to a doctor, Ella pleaded, knowing it was her Mother speaking through her mouth. Everything had been said already, but it was going to have to be repeated.

So as not to see his frown, Ella sent him text messages. *Are you going to see a doctor?* She dictated that question and waited for her phone to transcribe the words, but she trusted too much or got distracted and sent the text without checking how it had rendered her phrase. It transcribed wrong. *Ahí going ciudad.* She repeated the line, rounding out consonants and vowels, but it was even worse: *Ahí Cohen Chuck ciudad.*

But El didn't make an appointment with the doctor, because he always got home late or too tired and collapsed immediately onto the sofa. His eyelids swollen with exhaustion.

* * *

Carbon 14 disintegrates slowly, leaving a residue that allows time to be read in bones, El explains while he watches Ella down a *chupe de locos* and a soda. As if she didn't know about that isotope's radiometric properties. As if she didn't know that inside its atoms are six protons and eight neutrons charged with nuclear energy, plus the six electrons in the shell. As if she had no idea that its slow destruction allowed for the measurement, in any kind of matter, of the time Ella once dreamed of reformulating.

* * *

In its etymology an atom is indivisible, but in science an atom could always explode. It had to burst in order to give rise to something new.

An old cosmologist conjectured that after the big bang there must have been other, smaller explosions that produced infinite pocket universes scattered through space. Some empty and others saturated with matter, some eternal, others ephemeral, others that were expanding too quickly and violated the human laws of physics. But why would they be so different? Ella thought. Why was it only humans who were lucky enough to live in a space specially designed for them? A space, a planet, that humans seemed intent on destroying.

Life on earth was composed of 82 percent plants, 13 percent bacteria, and the remaining 5 percent included everything else. Of that everything else, only 0.01 percent was human. And still, that 0.01 percent was finishing off the other species. It was even finishing off itself.

* * *

The impact of the explosion had been distributed over his whole body in small wounds that were destroying him from the inside.

* * *

Do you have a nervous temperament? The doctor ran through his checklist of questions, looking out of the corner of his eye at El's forehead, crossed by a scar, El's still-wounded cheeks, his sliced ear. Nervous? he asked. Not especially.

I can see that you and I, says the gastroenterologist, reading the file through his glasses and peering at El over their frames. That you and I, he repeats, producing a startling smile, his fat cheeks crowding his eyelids from below. You and I. He starts over again, this doctor of astute eyes, because he keeps looking for the rest of the sentence among the words he has stored away in his cerebral archive. A phrase that doesn't sound ready-made. One that doesn't sound like he uses it with other patients. And this is the one he finds: Both of us, you and I, study the depths. You search beneath the earth for remains of bones, and I look in human cavities for the causes of your discomfort. It's the food, El ventures. It's heartburn, an ulcer about to start bleeding, insists Ella, who is there to translate what the gastroenterologist says, but El throws her a furious look and she goes quiet. Work has gotten very intense, El says, and again Ella interrupts, his job almost killed him. Now El squeezes the hand he is holding and Ella holds back a whimper. El coughs. The doctor raises his eyebrow, widens his almond-

74

shaped eyes, and blinks quickly, as though thinking something is going on between these two but he doesn't know what, and he doesn't know how to reply. Although maybe his compulsive blinking is nothing but a nervous tic, the visual proof that he's hiding something or will have something to say only once he's peered inside El's digestive apparatus.

* * *

Composite sketch portrait. Lips that cover *teeth pharynx trachea marrow*. Separated by the epiglottis, the esophagus down to the stomach's upper sphincter, the cardia, the incisura angularis, and the lower orifice that regulates drainage toward the narrow duodenum, then the thick colon followed by the last of the sphincters, the anus.

* * *

Idea for an ending. The philosopher refused to penetrate her darkest cavities. He would be forever convinced that Ella had left him for his lack of daring. That guy wasn't right for you, her Mother assured her, pleased without knowing why.

There were others who weren't right for her, but they were able to evade the maternal radar.

When El was about to meet her parents, Ella felt the need to tell him about the Mother's intractable vetos. To confide in El before introducing them. They were leaving customs, El exhausted by fever, faint from tiredness, wanting to throw himself into a bed after the trip. Now that we're here you're telling me this? and his question sizzles in the air, his eyebrows curl in displeasure. Those were other times, Ella says, sheepish. It was another existence of mine, other fears of my replacement Mother's. It wasn't necessary to defend that Mother who wasn't genetically hers, but she defended her anyway to save herself from the judgment El must be passing on them both. With his lips still twisted, El made her swear that never, not even after he died, would she tell her Mother what his defect was.

Let truths fall into black holes.

* * *

It's a reflex: El raises his hand to caress her cheek and Ella dodges it. She can't help it, her body has learned to sense an incoming blow. I've never laid a finger on you, El says, offended, shouting at her as if he were still deaf.

Blows, no. Shoes against the walls, very close to her face, when he loses his head. When the shoe gets too close to Ella, he throws it to the floor and locks himself in the bedroom.

El had dedicated his life to identifying bones in order to put an end to violence. That assertion, far from scaring or dissuading her, shone for seconds in her mind. It would be some time before she understood that he'd been referring to his own violence.

* * *

She spoke to the nighttime students, at that school that was only for boys, about the violence of galaxies that cannibalized one another, leaving only ruins. The milky way once had a sister galaxy that met an unexpected end when it was devoured by andromeda. Only the crumbs of the previous galaxy were left, she said, catching the students' attention.

* * *

When the semester ended, her shy thermodynamics professor drove her home, and on the way there he described his daily enemas. She still wonders if sharing about his hygiene habits was his way of wooing her.

* * *

If only she'd studied the periodic table hung in her classroom when she was fifteen. If only, instead of carving the chemical elements with a pin into the hexagonal sides of her pencil, or into the polystyrene pen tube. If only she hadn't copied on tests. But how could she have known then that each element corresponded to a solution to the quantum mechanics equation?

Did you know that the hole in the side of bic pens helps regulate pressure? Did you know they added a hole to the plastic cap so a person wouldn't choke if they swallowed it? El looks at her in horror.

* * *

She assumed El would rather not know, so she called her Father to tell him about the camera the size of a pill that would soon replace all those exams that ended in oscopy. The article didn't say whether the camera, once its intestinal voyage was over, would be reused.

And she spoke to her Father about an extraordinary asteroid that not only contained the most primitive matter in the universe, but also was completely *curiche coal black*, full of amino acids. And how do they know whether it's carbon or not? asked the Father, and Ella replied that they'd subjected the asteroid to a spectroscopy.

* * *

Together they read the instructions and dispel doubts as to how to prepare for that double exam that the cavity specialist is going to perform on him. Colonoscopy, below. Endoscopy, above. Together they understand that it isn't copy, but scopy, a visual examination.

And Ella wonders whether El's *defect insult catapult boot* would be seen in the exam, if it would be revealed or would remain forever a secret.

The instructions glued to the jar of that whitish concoction announce that the evacuation will be a process neither short nor simple but that, when followed to a T, the intestine will be left impeccable for observation. It sounds like a plumbing job, Ella comments with an impertinent smile. More like archaeology, El replies, as he scrupulously cleans his glasses.

* * *

His preparation consists of thinking back to torturous past procedures.

When they tied him to a cot and six hands held his head while the surgeon inserted a long anesthesia needle through the nostril of his pointy nose. When his body tensed up as if it were receiving an electric shock. When his lips twisted into a grimace. When his fallen face. When he shed theatrical sideways tears over the gloved fingers of the people who were holding him down. When they cut off the protuberance that had grown in there. When it smelled like burned meat.

Worse had been the operation on his herniated groin: to climb five flights with the freshly sutured cut and collapse into bed. The sharp saber wound when he sat on the toilet and confronted the task of pushing. High score on the scale of extreme pain.

But much worse was the free extraction of the four wisdom teeth embedded in his gums. They offered to enter him in a double-blind experiment, a painkiller and a placebo. Fifty percent likelihood of coming out of it unscathed. He didn't have a choice: he couldn't afford the surgery with painkillers and he agreed to have them strip him of his molars, the slight crack each time, the cotton in his gums. And they watched what happened without perceiving that he'd gotten the placebo, because El had signed a document in which he agreed to endure a little pain. And he wasn't sure how much was a little, but El was a man of his word.

Repeat the word pain a hundred times.

Repeat a hundred times: endure without a word.

Seventeen is the painful sum of all the operations he's accumulated in his record. If he had to return to those halls of martyrdom he would mark a 64 on the fear scale.

* * *

He had left that dentist who'd asked him to endure just a little bit more to avoid giving him anesthesia. With his mouth wide open and a buzzing machine inside, El was unable to defend himself. Since then he's brushed his teeth zealously, until his gums bleed, and he slides the dental floss between his molars as if committing hari-kari. In the future, he thinks, he'll never have to open his mouth for anyone.

Ella recommended his next dentist, though it's not so much a recommendation as an assurance that there will be anesthesia without any need to ask for it. That dentist now observes the molar enlarged on the screen. Now here's something I don't like, says the specialist, comparing the swollen root with one that is not. With a minuscule metal hammer he taps lightly on each of the molars and asks El if he can tell a difference. El feels none. He doesn't know. Doesn't answer.

That same dentist had shown Ella, on the screen, the infected nerve of her molar and a root curved ninety degrees that looked difficult to reach, even with fine tools and kung fu moves. He'd never seen anything like it, he exclaimed through his mask. An anatomical variation like that. It could be left alive and dying, and he was referring to the crooked root but also to the molar's owner, who was Ella. Alive but dying. And he asked her permission to use those photos at some dental conference. He filled her with anesthesia and while her gums lost feeling the dentist wanted to know what her previous dentist had done with the coiled angle of that still-living root. He put arsenic on it to kill the nerve, Ella stammered, feeling her tongue swelling and her voice thicken. Arsenic? The dentist of the present knew nothing of such outdated practices. And how did the arsenic work out for you? She described a jaw whipped by electric currents.

To think that the Twins slept, snored, laughed with their mouths open in the dentist chair. They were immune to the noise of the machines and the torture they supposedly inflicted.

* * *

Ella didn't doubt her colleague, the math teacher, when she told her during a break how many dentists she'd had to pay to free her from a toothache. The x-rays didn't show any alteration and three dentists in a row told her that the throbbing pain would pass. If the image didn't show the ache it was because it wasn't there. She was clenching her teeth too much, they were worn down. The dentists gave her muscle relaxers that kept her from articulating her complaints. They stuck a nauseating paste in her mouth to make a mold of her teeth, a mouth guard that brought no relief either. The fourth dentist sent her to the psychiatrist, but Ella's colleague didn't give up: hers was no psychosomatic or psychiatric problem; it was eating away at her gum. Overcome by the extreme reality of her pain, she demanded that the umpteenth dentist pull the molar. It came out easily: the roots were rotten, and so was the piece of jaw that went with the tooth into the garbage.

Was it her Mother or Father who said that only after ruling out physical causes could one venture a cause of another origin? Was it her Mother who warned her that doctors tended to distrust the pain of women? That many died because a doctor sent them home without attending to them? And which parent had assured her there was a high percentage of healthy people in every waiting room insisting they were sick? Their complaints exhausted the doctors, who couldn't ignore them anymore, now that the patients could sue them.

* * *

Hypochondria story. In ancient times it referred to an area *beneath* or *hipo* the rib *cartilage*, or *condria*, and was a digestive disorder of the *liver spleen nervous gallbladder*. Centuries later the same hypochondria was used to describe a melancholy disorder marked by indigestion and stomach ailments that were hard to pinpoint.

It was her Father who told her that highly educated people did nothing but complain, and that those in poverty, on the other hand, could stand more, much more, or maybe they felt less. He also said that distraction could be the best medicine, but that same medicine could be lethal if one denied all symptoms. Because pain is the awareness of being alive. One has to be a little dead or a little deaf in order for the body to rest.

* * *

Find out whether El had kept the teeth his gums had lost over the course of his lifetime. El gives her a questioning look. He kept teeth only from the cadavers he had to identify. But Ella saved hers, the ones that had fallen out and the ones that had been extracted, the many molars with cavities; she wanted to see what would happen to them later. She also kept the molds of her jaw taken by the orthodontist at the clinic her Mother had taken her to in order to straighten her crooked smile, which never did get in line. The orthodontist stuck his bare fingers into her mouth, fit braces on, and tightened the screws on her jaw, though Ella felt that the metal thread stretched out through her bones and ended coiled in her spine.

She couldn't chew for days.

* * *

Now she looked at the food growing cold on El's plate. His fork turning over the rice that he never raised to his mouth. What are you thinking about, Posi? Ella asked, trying to be supportive. Are you at the dig site? He laid his silverware on the table. I've got a gut feeling I can't get rid of, El answered, and he lit the cigarette that was his only food. His stomach's intuitive intelligence was telling him that the government was protecting the extremist groups that were implicated in the mass-grave investigation.

Your gut feeling scares me, your heartburn scares me, your bloated stomach, but those people scare me more, Ella insisted, as she saw the color leave his face. El closed his eyes and stayed silent. You're risking your hide: that unshakable certainty now came from her own gut.

* * *

Psychiatry had realized that the body had an alternate nervous system: the chemicals used to fix troubled brains brought on adverse effects in the digestive apparatus. The gastroenterologist who was going to look inside El had explained to them that the gut has a brain of its own. He'd raised his eyelids with effort, and they saw his lacerating eyes open wide as he informed them that the brain in the guts has just as many neuroreceptors and neurotransmittors as the brain in the head.

* * *

A lone cabin in a vibrant clearing, with a violet lake and falcons flying over in the succulent evening air. It's growing dark, they're rocked by the warm breath of the stars. With her head resting on his hairy stomach, she stares up at the uneasy lights of the firmament that reach them from an obsolete time. And, thinking that El is listening, she points out to him, from the hanging swing, a very bright star that in the past had been thought to be two. A binary star, she said, alpha centari, which is really three stars—there's another one that's very small and close by that can't be seen with the naked eye. That would be a great subject for a thesis, don't you think? But El isn't listening to her; he stands up and clutches his head in his hands as if someone were howling into his ears. Did the whistling come back? He shakes his head, no, no, the whistling never left, it's blowing softly, but this is an intense headache; his chin sinks to his chest and his hair sticks up between his fingers. Can I bring you something? Ella asks, now sitting up, alert now, thinking that his blood pressure must have risen, going over what medicines she'd put in the portable pharmacy that was her backpack. She thinks back to the dirt path without *moon help croaking frogs*, and she remembers that phone coverage tends to be spotty in this kind of backwater, where they've come to take a break from murdered workers and murderers, from neighbors partying every Friday.

This alone at last could turn out to be a lonely ending, Ella thinks, trying not to think so much, all the time, but even if she shuts off her head, her innards are still there, *neurasthenic neurotic gut.*

Her mind was never quiet. No mind ever was.

* * *

And it was worse to remember that uncle Ella never met, the one who woke his wife to complain of an unbearable headache, and got up for a painkiller but never had time to find it.

But a severe headache isn't always an aneurism, she told herself.

Repeat a hundred times, not always, not always.

* * *

Rather than thinking about so much misfortune, why don't you focus on your thesis?

What have you done all day? That was another of his scathing questions. Ella knew that El knew she got distracted thinking about other things. She pretended to be deaf.

* * *

Ferocious headaches everyone had gotten used to. It happened so often: her Actor friend's boyfriend would get a migraine and at the last minute cancel on their plans to go to the club. Then they'd go just the two of them, Ella and the Actor, who was still performing then. Neither of them anticipated that the boyfriend would have a stroke, that a hole would have to be drilled into his head to drain the blood that was putting pressure on the capsule of his skull.

That soon he'd be found lying on the sticky floor of his apartment. He took too many pills, said her Actor friend, who was working in a theater ticket booth. By then they weren't together anymore, but they still saw each other sometimes, like old brothers.

When he learned of his son's death, the boyfriend's father suffered a similar collapse. They were men of fragile arteries and high blood pressure, and panic attacks were particularly dangerous for them, said Ella's Father, as if sadness were a function of the organs.

* * *

The ancients thought that sadness came from a malign alignment of the stars.

* * *

El dreamed again about the old neighbor who'd been buried weeks before, or maybe cremated. He moved his headstone aside, the mouth open in a mute scream, and in went El, into the howl, sliding down the esophagus toward a stomach full of acid. But, blind in those murky waters, he couldn't find the exit and he tripped over some bones that he recognized as his own. At the other end of the sheet Ella had the passing, drowsy impression that he was babbling a string of words that rhymed with *sorry sin sacrum*, and she thought he was dreaming about her.

* * *

The Father often told the story of when he was in his thirties and a worker came into his hospital, groaning. My thinking bone hurts, doctor, said the worker, taking off his cap and pointing to his temple.

But her Father's osseous knowledge was limited, much as he insisted on discussing bones with El, making every effort to contradict him. To give him lessons about forensic studies. But you aren't a bone specialist, El protested one day, tired of the Father's disdain. When it comes to living bones I know a lot more than you, replied the Father, watching El rise indignantly from the table. Ella stood up, too, and left the Father alone, drumming his fingernails on the tablecloth.

I've had it up to here with your Father, he told Ella. I just can't stand his arrogance. It builds up, like an allergy, it affects me more and more. Now you're sounding just like him, Ella retorted, smiling, and El smiled, too, in resignation. Your Father is contagious.

* * *

You were screaming, Ella said one night, shaking him awake. El opened his eyes like a blind man and shoved Ella's hands from his shoulders, then jumped from the bed and stared at her in fear. I was strangling you, he said, and he rubbed his hands on the sheet.

* * *

The day of the double probe was approaching. Ella started to think about what they were going to put into El between his lips and legs. She thought about El's body, but she ended up remembering that of the man she'd never managed to love.

Intimate portrait, dead of night. Ella announced her departure to the man, though she had nowhere to go. All she could leave was the room they shared, and wait for the next morning to move. She went into the small room next door, and while she was taking off her dress and hanging it over the back of a chair, the man forced the door and gave her a shove that knocked the wind out of her. She saw him unbuckle his belt and she turned her face to keep from seeing his body so close, upright, assailing her on the futon. That's how he tried to dissuade her. The man releasing his rage onto her, insulting her, biting her, spitting in her eyes. He kept coming at her and Ella knew the blows would grow harder and they did, but she felt that she no longer felt anything, that she'd come unstuck from herself and all of her became an arm stretched out and a hand that fumbled and found, on a nightstand or in a drawer or on the floor, a *stick dildo dried paintbrush*. Possessed by a strength she'd been honing for centuries and by her clenched fist, she stuck that rod into him, from behind. She pushed it until she felt that whatever was in her hand had disappeared inside. Her fingers strangled by a rectum.

An object that could have been a fork or a coffee spoon, a knife left carelessly beneath the window.

Because even before that night another man had come at her. In a bend of the past. In her own country. She'd been leaving a party in the moonless early morning, heels tapping softly on uneven pavement. Her feet hurt; she leaned against a wall while she took off her shoes and wondered where she'd parked her car. She was rubbing an ankle when a stranger came out of nowhere and pushed her against the climbing vines, not speaking, not threatening her, his breathing agitated in her ear as if he were more scared than she was, though it wasn't fear he was feeling. He held her neck, pressed her face against the *wall crushed snails warm slime*. On her thighs some rough fingers multiplied and tore at her underwear, went into her like slippery worms, covered her nose so she'd open her mouth. Fingers that entered her *dry open lip-full* mouth and muffled her scream with her own underpants while the stranger fit his body behind her.

* * *

If she'd found a spoon. Some sharp scissors. A knife to murder that memory. But there are moments that no weapon can destroy.

Nor were there tools that could destroy her older brother's rage.

* * *

Take refuge in dance clubs full of men who only *seek kiss punish* other men.

Early morning, tired of dancing, her Actor friend drives them home in his small red hot rod. They're crossing the city. The Actor's boyfriend is in the passenger seat, and in the back seat Ella leans against the shoulder of her Friend, who has just become a doctor. They speed through an intersection strewn with glass. Three cars recently crashed, up on the sidewalk. Stop, stop, shrieks the Friend, a specialist in urgent care. And the car brakes and Ella and the Friend run back to the site of the accident.

They're left in the car, those men without women.

Red flashing lights illuminate the street.

And they hear a voice wailing. The man in the truck is screaming about his ankle but the ER Friend keeps going. Pain isn't a priority, she says breathlessly, pain is life, it's consciousness and possible recovery. There's an old man standing up and staggering, and as the Friend passes she orders him to lie down on the pavement. The corner starts to fill with disheveled neighbors wakened by the crash, and Ella, more awake than anyone, helps her Friend, ordering them with a newfound authority to clear the sidewalk, call an ambulance, bring a flashlight for the doctor in charge. And for the men to pull out the wounded who are still in those accordioned cars. Hold their heads, don't let their necks bend, the fragile backbone.

Protocol is to find the fallen. Check their vital signs in two or three words. Conscious. Alert. Oriented. Because a pair of open eyes is never a guarantee. Because breathing means little. What day is it. What year. What month. Who is the president. And if they respond correctly they must be abandoned ipso facto to look for those who can't respond, those who are at risk but can still be saved.

Abandon those who can still complain and the hopelessly wounded, the irreversible cases.

The girl was imprisoned under the metal and had to be extracted without damaging her spine, which was already broken. Lay her on the pavement, unbutton her pants. Check neurological signs.

In her dilated pupils shone the distant red light and the white light, close-up and devastating, from the flashlight the Friend turned on to see if her pupils responded. She put a knuckle between her breasts and dug it in to hurt her. Because a live wounded person, even if they're unconscious, would try to get away from that stabbing pain. The girl barely cringed and moved her elbows, and instead of protecting herself, she balled up her fists facing outward, like an articulated doll's.

And that head, attached to the body as though by a spring, in perpetual motion.

That *hoarse guttural dissonant* gasp, that panting of narrow gills. Pharynx—that's to say wrong, because live breath comes from the larynx, her Friend would say later, light-years away from that clear night. That night the Friend decreed there was no hope for the girl. Dead? Ella asked, disconcerted, but she's still breathing. Breathing erratically, the Friend corrected. That rattle comes from brain death.

The Father, who had been the Friend's internal medicine professor, would confirm her diagnosis.

* * *

The Friend had asked if she could spend the night with Ella. Her roommates had gone to the beach and she was afraid of going home alone, of putting the key in the lock alone and fumbling on the wall for a light switch. She had never overcome her fear of the dark leftover from the closet where her grandmother made her hide during the police raids in search of her parents. In there she couldn't see those men who always repeated the same thing: where are they, where've you got them—as if her grandmother had swallowed them, as if the grandmother wasn't wondering the same thing, as if she didn't want to ask them the same question— open your mouth, you old cunt, we'll cut out your tongue for being an accessory, and they'd shake the grandmother, kick her until she lost consciousness.

* * *

El swallowed half of the intestinal wash that started right away to do its plumbing job. They both suffered the excremental burst. El was emptied out, Ella stared into space, diverting her thoughts.

* * *

And though it was nearly dawn when they were dropped off at Ella's apartment, they couldn't fall asleep. They'd gotten into bed with a chamomile tea to shake off the tragedy of the dead girl. Then they

90

heard steps above their heads. Someone was walking on the roof—more than one person. And the balcony was long and narrow and the locks on the glass doors were rusted. The Friend grabbed a steak knife from the drawer in the kitchen and Ella, equally afraid of the footsteps and the metal blade, called the police. And a cop came with a laughing air and let fall a Ladies, how many drinks have you had? Quiet, Ella blurted as if addressing an impertinent child. Listen. The steps were above their heads again. And the cop called reinforcements, who came immediately, and they all went up to the roof, but there was no one there. And the cops smiled ironically, and both girls were still in nightgowns, and Ella asked them again to lower their voices so they could hear, all of them together in the silence that followed, the creaking footsteps of those bodies that weren't there.

* * *

A body is always somewhere, El observes, furrowing his brow.

That wasn't true. A body could vanish, Ella thinks, hating all those professors who stopped answering the messages she sent asking for help with her dissertation. One by one, they'd evaporated.

* * *

It's no longer a state secret that the cadavers belong to recent immigrants and that they aren't the only ones: others are discovered during the excavation for the foundation of a building, and in a mass grave beside the river with *shovels swastikas knives banners* proclaiming death to migrants. Shit, El says, twisted up by cramps, it's happening before our eyes! Breaking news! And though he had already swallowed half the liquid and was in and out of the bathroom, he decided to postpone the exam. He couldn't be absent the whole next day if his boss was still away.

***

El opened a bottle of wine and poured two glasses. He asked her to sit down, he wanted to say something. Ella ran her hand through her hair and raised her eyebrows and sat down without knowing how to look at him, because she was afraid it was going to hurt. I'm all ears, she said, not daring to pick up the glass. Why don't we leave? El asked. *¿A dónde?* she said, realizing what he was suggesting, that they go back to the country of the past, and she asked, to live? Certainly not to die, El parried, smiling moodily. This country is finished and it's going to finish us. Ella looked at him in astonishment: I don't have any future in my country of the past.

But that wasn't true either.

The only true thing was that Ella was starting to doubt.

***

El traveled to the capital, and Ella stayed working more on her classes than on research for her thesis. She kept wasting *human oneiric cosmic* time but she wondered, to excuse herself from work, just who could dive into astral abstractions with all the terrifying news going on around them. All the victims were, like her, immigrants.

***

She was still alone in the apartment and in her manuscript when the doorbell rang: it was a scientist from El's team who lived in the neighborhood. She didn't recognize his voice and at first she thought he was drunk, but he was asking for a painkiller, the strongest Ella had. He mentioned the medicine chest, and she understood that El had described it to his inner circle. What else had he told them? And though she didn't know the man, she let him up, waited on the threshold for the scientist who was now introducing himself with an unintelligible first and last name. Come in, she said, watching him clutch his bearded jaw with one hand. The dentist had filled one molar and broken another, but the scientist had realized only once the anesthesia wore off and the dentist's office was closed. The pain was unspeakable: he couldn't open his mouth. Ella called her Mother to ask if she'd left any extraordinary painkillers in the first-aid kit. Of course, her Mother said eagerly. A vial of dipyrone, a gram that she would have to inject for the scientist. But this injection wouldn't be like the vaccines Ella had learned to give herself. She would have to inject his gluteus. That was the word the Mother used with Ella, and then Ella used it with the scientist who was lying on his boss's bed. He'd have to pull down his pants and underwear, and he obeyed, he surrendered to her clumsy hands while she filled the syringe and flicked it with a fingernail to get any air bubbles out. She was slapping him so he would relax and the *hypnotic hammer fork needle* wouldn't hurt so much, because that was what her Mother, still on the phone, had suggested. The Mother was telling her to divide the gluteus into four parts and inject the outer upper quadrant, that she should avoid the ilium, and if the needle did hit it, she should withdraw. That was absurd, it was impossible to touch bone, the Father would say later, because the scientific ass was round and hairy and adult and the bone was sunk very deep beneath muscle. But Ella didn't know that, and, afraid of striking skeleton, she didn't dare force the needle. She rested the point against the flesh and pushed slowly, does it hurt much? and he let out a groan that was hard to decipher. Ten or twelve? Ella said, knowing the scientist didn't understand the question, that he couldn't answer, tell me to stop if I'm hurting you, but she said it with no intention of stopping, pressing harder until the syringe went into the skin and the needle disappeared and Ella could finally give him the painkiller.

93

The word painkiller, a hundred times in a row, and the scientist pulling up pants wrinkled like he'd slept in them all night.

The bearded scientist had already left, sending greetings to his boss, by the time El returned from his last supper with the conference goers in the capital. El didn't want that political position that was dragging on, a temporary position where he had to keep his head down and say yes or suffer the consequences he was already suffering, skinny as a dagger. A twitchy eyelid. The whine in his ear was driving him crazy. He was full of acid after an extremely tense meeting and didn't like what Ella was saying to him, thinking he'd find it funny. One of these days you'll get arrested, he said sharply, spraying her with spittle. What if my scientist was allergic to whatever you gave him and he'd died on you here, right here? On my rug. On my bed, did you say? On my very own bed! In my house, in my building, in my place, the only thing I have; his voice had turned sulfurous and was starting to burn Ella. He was throwing cushions to the floor, kicking them mercilessly against the wall. He picked up a shoe and shook it while he looked at her as though deranged, but he stopped, threw it to the floor, went into the bedroom with a loud slam of the door.

He opened it again and walked down the hall to lock himself in the kitchen. Like a man committing suicide, he drank all the liquid left in the bottle.

* * *

Ella would rather he'd hit her. The blow would bring his body closer to hers, would awaken a caress, would end the silence they had sunk into. To feel his fist burning on her face seemed better than his distance.

* * *

94

They ask him to lie on his side, they open the robe at his back, ask him if he minds having some medical students as witnesses. That's when he remembers his precarious doctoral life, his life as an intern before his present life, and he whispers almost asleep that no, he doesn't mind, because he manages to think that if they see only his ass they will never recognize his face.

* * *

He surrenders blindly to the observation of a neutral eye.

* * *

And while she waits for him outside, Ella pulls the lid off her jar of memories and is hit by the smell of aspirin, the sight of the green boxes her Father handed out to relatives and patients. They were the free samples he got for appearing in a commercial recommending their use. The Firstborn would say he had no interest in watching the Father promote optimum blood circulation and women in labor bleeding to death. Ella had never believed her Father was responsible for what happened. And at the evening hour when the entire country tuned in to watch the telenovela, Ella sat on the sofa eager for commercials: During that interruption the Father would appear in his immaculate smock. With the stethoscope around his neck. With his hair slicked back and the little mustache he would later shave off.

She was pulled from this memory by the nurse who passed her in a white burka. All eyes, lined, enormous, and startling, which her Father wouldn't have seen as inquisitive or intimidating, but rather as the eyes of a woman suffering from hyperthyroidism. And she fanned herself with a magazine in the waiting room until El emerged from the end of the hall and approached, teetering, a little dizzy but already dressed, and he sat down beside her, put a hand on her knee, and gave her a How's it going, Electron? All charged, Ella said. You, Posi? And El smiled sadly and she knew that they must have seen nothing more than an excess of restless gases and dangerous acid, which they could hopefully calm with medication.

And behind him came the indiscreet innard-delving doctor, now without gloves, smelling of lavender. His face shone above the pile of papers he deposited between them as he took a seat. They were portraits of El's internal cavities. The channel of his anus surrounded by that double muscular ring, the striated thickening of the rectum. Ella had sent him to see a doctor and now she was the one seeing El in successive color copies, the soft pink lustrous crannies where her eyes got lost. It was powerful, the certainty that she was getting to know him. The place that filtered the air he breathed and from where each word emerged, vibrating; the place where his screams were born. And the doctor distracted her by showing them *glands hemorrhoids cloves* that were the seat of the nervous system, sympathetic, somatic, and parasympathetic. And antipathetic, Ella thought, but that adjective wasn't for the doctor, because this specialist was all warmth and goodwill, while El was no longer the person he was when they met. She thought about hatred, the explosion, about fear, about the enigma of the skeletal remains and the lives that came before them. That's what Ella was thinking about and maybe El was, too, that maybe with time everything would be restored, but maybe not, because there in the night the stupid stars still hung and sprinkled calcium over the universe.

milky way

* past imperfect *

It was a cancerous family, or it had been. Many had died already, and the others were doing what they could to forget what it was they'd died of.

To forget, for example, that cancer is woven silently into tissue. Inside. Beneath. Around. That malignant cells orbit indiscernibly in blood and sometimes they are the blood itself. And that pain doesn't always sound the alarm, or not always in time.

Opening the heavy car door she felt a pinch on one side of her breast. She slipped her hand under her coat and jacket and blouse, under her bra; her fingers palpated and she knew there was something there. Rooted. Dense. Deadly? She'd found so many hard and painful lumps before and they were never anything. And she got into the car remembering that she had just posed for the hospital radiologist and that her backlit portrait was clean. But she knew that an old and fibrous chest like hers was a thick cloth that rays couldn't always pierce.

* * *

The Mother called from the past to give Ella all the news at once. A tumor throbbed in her breast like a small heart. A tumor they were going to remove. Biopsy of lymphatic nodes. The dose of chemo still to be determined and the radiation sessions. Her mouth would fill up with sores. Her leukocytes would go down, of course. And she said it as though speaking of another doctor's patient or a dead brother-in-law or the *aunts nieces enemies of friends* upon whom no compassion was bestowed.

Of course her hair would fall out, from eyebrows to toes. She was going to be balder than balls, declared the Mother, who was afraid of everything but crude words. She was going to need a wig, or maybe she'd use a scarf.

And the word scarf opened in Ella a portal, and through it peered the woman whose eyebrows were drawn on in pencil, lips lined, that gaunt woman strolling the muddy streets of Ella's memory with her head wrapped in the strips of a rag.

Sometimes words shook her past.

Sometimes they were spells that Ella repeated in case they could bring about a desired result. Abracadabra had been conceived by the gnostics as a shield against cancer.

* * *

Ella went out to her city's center, that swarm of tourists moving slowly down the avenues, that whisper of *voices fingers security cam-*

eras, sheer skyscrapers crisscrossed by pulses of neon, and she entered the university library that stretched out through miles of underground tunnels. She found aisles PS169, PR605, PQ8098, RA644, where motion sensors turned on artificial lights over the shelves. She'd never been in that part of the library, because she'd never looked for the stories of women with cancer that now she wanted to read. There were hundreds of books, death diaries, terminal novels, testimonies of sons and daughters returning to bury their mothers before the cadaver got cold, to warm one last misery in their memories.

A wave of light blinded her when she reemerged with a stack of books balanced in her arms.

In those books she found drawers full of centenary objects, photo albums of cancerous mothers, the shameless scrutiny of intimate letters that no one should read, the sniffing of a perfume still alive in someone's clothes. All the things that now would have no use. Boxes of dried-out makeup. Dull razor blades. Shaggy hairbrushes. Moth-eaten dresses that would get tossed into the garbage, where they'd be better off. Where they would finally disintegrate, instead of being embalmed in the eternity of some trunk.

* * *

There was no room to store things, *nothing none no viperous tongues*, apologized the Mother when the Girl Twin asked what she'd done with the Grandmother's x-rays.

Ella would explain to the annoyed Girl Twin that the Mother had done the same thing with Ella's mom's x-rays, which her Father had stored in large white envelopes in a drawer. The Mother had thrown the osseous portraits into a dumpster somewhere along with all the black-and-white photos, but she didn't really say the part about the dumpster because it was only speculation. She couldn't prove that the Mother had made the photos of her genetic mother disappear that way, along with all the childhood toys that might remind Ella of a Motherless time.

Kill off the genetic mother with her forgetting. Ella had never seen her face and had ended up erasing it.

*　*　*

It was in a used bookstore that Ella found the novel about the woman with cancer, delusional and devoted as her own Mother, who looked at the spots on her chest x-rays stuck to the mirror and saw the immaculate being who would work the miracle of curing her. But the Virgin's appearance was only a mirage.

*　*　*

The Mother needed to confirm that Ella would be willing to return to the past for a few days or a couple of weeks. To keep your Father company, she said, as she always did, her voice going a little higher, putting the Father first though the Mother was right there, just behind him, waiting for her as for the prodigal daughter Ella could never be.

Come back to your country. The Mother would slip in provocations like that. Ella replied, this is my country, too, for now. Or she'd say, I've never left. She couldn't use El as protection, because he hadn't yet appeared. The Mother kept on, impassive, we'll find you a guy here, not understanding that Ella had met only the wrong guys and now didn't want to risk anything with anyone. She couldn't even imagine one existed who didn't have fists in his pockets, one who wouldn't cause pain, and anyway she wasn't there to look for a man. Her only mission was to find a habitable planet so she could formulate a doctoral hypothesis, but liquid water still hadn't been found on any planet, no organic material, no energy source, that was her only concern, that's what Ella told her, but the Mother didn't listen. The Mother repeated that she should return to the past, where she would find a suitable man. Ella set the phone on the table and let her talk, only occasionally lifting it back to her ear and emitting an mm-hmm, yes, could be, so, without rhyme or reason, and the Mother, suspecting she'd lost her, raised her voice over the phone. Because how was she going to find a man with those strange girlfriends of hers surrounding her, penning her in and keeping her from looking around, from having a little fun, from getting dressed up a little, never letting her, hugging her to the point of suffocation in the photos they took, those faces with eyes sunken from lack of sleep, always around or beside or above, blinding her with artificial office light? They were always studying together, solving formulas or doubting their own conjectures, eating little because a life of study was a life of hunger, of smoking too much, together, and drinking coffee until ulcers opened up, and of staying awake all night, staying to sleep *together disheveled damp shiver* on mattresses full of bedbugs, the Mother said inaudibly, wrinkling her nose a little, squinting her eyes, all those girlfriends who always wore pants and short hair and who scared everyone off with hypotheses that they would take an eternity to prove. Nor did the Mother approve of her male classmates, of whom there were many more, though they were already starting to thin out, all single, all sweaty, dirty, badly shaven, stuck like monks to the god of their screens and growing potbellies of bread and baloney. They were a sect of studious men losing their sight and their teeth. The Mother said this and laughed uproariously at her conjectures, because of course she'd never met any of those monks of physics much less the nuns of science, those girls with furrowed brows marching toward their futures.

Ella was getting left behind, lost in the stratosphere.

They were at their regular bar when her colleagues let her know that there was a rumor about her. That she was an intruder in the physics field. That she was lying to them when she said she'd lost all her work from recent years, that her expensive computer had filled up with a replicant virus, that the pricey repairs didn't work, it still gave the *404 error please restart*, or else the 403 forbidden error. Those were nothing but clumsy excuses, they rolled with laughter at her, at Ella, who was paralyzed with a glass of wine in her hand, realizing that they'd been talking behind her back for months, listening to them tell her now, in person, face-to-face and with frank condescension, that her only error had been to believe she had some talent for hard sciences. The only thing she was good at was speculation, said the friend Ella had believed was her closest. Because, added the traitor, the ideas that came out of her mouth were truly unheard-of. Her logic. Her words. They were good for a laugh, she said, laughing scornfully. And the other girls agreed, raised their glasses, toasted to her health before leaving her there with her spirit crushed, as they took off all together on their meteoric careers.

Ella would stop showing up at the university, she would stop sending greetings to the women she'd thought were her friends, or to the men she couldn't trust either. She would keep the hope of finishing her doctorate alight, but that fire would gradually grow dimmer. One professor after another excused themselves from advising on her thesis. 410 error, Ella thought: professor unavailable.

* * *

Without planning it, *birds in her head climbing up her legs*, she would meet the man of her future in the city of the past. She'd seen him from a distance, through her dirty glasses, but there he was, on the podium, in blue jeans, a white shirt without cufflinks and no jacket, gesticulating with his hands and tics of his language as he gave a master class at the museum of memory. Ella would raise her hand to ask a question at the end. She would try to catch his attention, see if he smiled, see how he talked to someone who wasn't an expert in his subject. What Ella was wondering was what kind of man El might be.

A man with an open mind and a book under his arm.

* * *

That man of the future hadn't appeared on her horizon yet and Ella kept the receiver pressed against her ear, against the Mother's voice that went on saying, as though to itself and with the worst of intentions, *breathing dust queen bee*, darling, listen to me, here you could find someone, settle down, teach at just one school with just one decent contract, and not in all those little schools. And Ella corrected her, schools, mom, they're not little—public without contempt. The Mother wouldn't let herself be interrupted, finish that thing you're doing, that, that whatever it is you're writing, how much longer is it going to take?

It would take Ella a while to realize that the Mother blamed El for keeping her far from her family, from her country. The Mother believed El was preventing her from finishing her thesis, so he could keep her with him.

* * *

Her daughter was very clever, the Mother would say, swollen with contempt toward those robust and incredulous secretaries in her hospital who imagined the doctor's daughter writing an esoteric tome. Habitable planets and later the black holes sounded less like science and more like fiction. One of the secretaries whispered behind the Mother's back that she thought she was just the cat's pajamas. Oh cute! cried a secretary who'd just started.

Tomcats, backs arched, mounting apathetic females. Those words came to her head because that's how she was starting to feel: like a cat, the male and female simultaneously.

And the reminder that she hadn't started her manuscript, her *quantic gravitational thermodynamic or what have you* book, made her hair stand on end, arched her back with multiplied vertebrae, burned her pink and meaty throat, dried out her corneas.

* * *

I already told you, mom, how many times, mom, a thesis takes time. And she had to write it in the city of the present because in her preterit country the thing Ella studied had no future.

Future, future, what do you know about the future? grumbled the Mother, looking indignantly at the palm of her hand.

How can there be no future here? jeered the Firstborn, looking at her sideways one afternoon. Under arid northern skies, observatories were popping up all over, the interstellar telescopes, continued her brother, that brother who remembered the sky only when it was raining and his bones creaked and rattled. They're just collecting the past of the cosmos there, it's nothing but *data entropy objects to identify*, Ella said, and she got up from the table, sick of giving explanations not even she fully understood.

Only once had she ventured up into the most arid hills, the most barren mountains, where the sky was transparent and the light so perfect it was like the stars arrived early, or like they never left the observatory's endless night. She'd gone out to see from close up what she had conjectured from so far away. That telescopic contemplation had made her dizzy, made her stomach retch, and she'd left without telling anyone she couldn't look. Not even her Father.

* * *

Those observatories penetrating the night.

Those earthly observatories were getting left in the past. The future belonged to satellites launched into space to determine the *magnitude distance parallactic revolution* of the stars. The satellites would gather the anatomical data of the milky way in the form of ones and zeros, which computers would translate into a map of the stars.

The Firstborn noticed his sister's rapid blinking, and his lips curled.

* * *

She called her Father to hear straight from his mouth what the prognosis was. The Father, grayer than usual, more stoic, less convincing than usual, said it was all about dodging obstacles in this sack race of life.

The Father didn't mention the possibility of death. Only the Mother did. They shouldn't think about that, countered the Father, and the Mother replied that they didn't need to think about it, death would be keeping them all in mind. But sometimes their roles were reversed and it was the Father who named death, while the Mother chose survival.

* * *

A mental mechanism keeps us from imagining the moment of our own death, because if it were possible to imagine that moment, the *defenselessness orphanhood flat encephalogram*, the anxiety would hasten the end.

The Mother's mother had always been afraid of dying, but somewhere along the way she had shed that fear. She never got the chance to tell them where.

* * *

The surgeon friend who had removed her Father's appendix had just come from operating on a terminal patient. He'd cut. Opened the man up. Saw that the cancer had spread. Instead of gutting and emptying the patient, the surgeon sewed him up carefully and waited for him to come out of anesthesia to send him off into the few sorry months he had left. He watched the man leave the hospital, dejected. Years later, it was the Father who told Ella how it all ended, how the surgeon friend reencountered the patient he'd given up for dead. Hi, doctor, cried the dead man in the elevator. Do you remember me?

Spontaneous remission is what that's called. It can happen; the immune system reactivates and takes care of those vile cells. But those are extremely rare cases, said the Mother.

* * *

How many times would she tell El this story that he would have preferred not to hear?

* * *

Esperar: Ella dictates into the phone to find out what becomes of the infinitive wait in her other language. *It's better at. Yes pay Dad.*

Cuántos días became *when does the ass* and *what does the S*. It all depended on how it was pronounced into the phone.

How many days could they wait for her while she found someone to substitute in her classes? Ella had already used all her vacation days, and this leave would have to be requested with a forced face of extenuating circumstances, explaining that emergencies existed in an alternate dimension of time.

* * *

Don't panic, she told her students on her last day before taking a week off to be with the Mother in her surgery. Don't be scared, she repeated, our black hole, unlike others farther away, is largely asleep, she told them, quiescent, she said, we'll all be dead before it wakes up and devours us.

* * *

She noticed the outside of the house needed a coat of paint. In the front yard were trees no one had pruned in a long time, and the yellowed grass was strewn with hungry birds pecking at its roots. And the Mother who opens the front door no longer looks like the one Ella knows: this one is different, again another mother, in a long white nightgown. She's the depleted version of herself, *frayed thinned grayed ghost*. Ella knows she could lose her, lose her again for good. She holds on to her body and won't let go.

Touch here, her Mother says, moving out of the embrace. Do you feel that?

The thing that lived inside the Mother and was also the Mother.

The thing that could someday grow inside Ella.

Sometime later and still thinking how at any moment that tumor could be hers, Ella asked El to touch her breasts. To squeeze them hard, handle them, dig his fingers into them. Do you feel anything? El stopped, looked in disgust at the naked torso he had just kissed: I can't like this.

Ella looked at El as if she knew he was going to hurt her, and didn't care.

It was only a matter of time before the first blow came, and yet it never came.

* * *

Hurry, grumbled the Mother, because the two half sisters were moving slowly on their way to the appointment with the plastic surgeon. Do we have to help you choose? asked the Girl Twin, taking the measure of the Mother's breasts out of the corner of her eye, the scarf coiled around her neck like a rabbit. Ella squeezed her elbow to distract the sister, who was staring at them now, at those maternal breasts, while the specialist assessed them with a measuring tape and then weighed them. Advertising his art, the surgeon presented them with a tray of possible silicone replacements in all sizes. He'd have them on hand in case of a complete removal.

Can I film this? asked the Girl Twin, whom the surgeon had just caught filming.

They were perfect breasts, inhuman breasts, and the Girl Twin sighed over the images now stored in her camera. Breasts she would show to her Boy Twin later. Do you think I should have mine reduced? she'd ask him, and her brother would say, touching them with his eyes, that her breasts were the nicest. Of the three women in his life, the Girl Twin was the one with the biggest chest, the most prone to gravitational pull.

***

Speculation about a diseased breast. How much does a breast weigh? A kilo? Half? More? Was one breast always heavier and more cantankerous than the other? And how much did its tumor weigh? What was it made of? The same stuff, of course. Fat, skin, some glands with first and last names. Areolas. Nipples. Lactiferous ducts. Cells identical to themselves multiplying their effort to destroy her.

***

Portrait of a woman whose nipple full of sarcoma is pulled off. Is a mutilated breast still a breast? Is a woman without breasts still a woman? The old woman who is the Mother feels like a half woman now, but Ella has seen *men simians cetaceans* with and without breasts who have still looked to her like what they were.

She'd been looking on her computer at nudes of women who'd chosen to stay flat after a mastectomy. One had tattooed flowers over her scars, another wore a tie hanging over her nakedness and sported a coy mustache. Their bodies stylized for glossy paper, Ella thought, saving the article that she wouldn't let her Mother read.

***

And there they were, gathered again in a hospital room, waiting for the Mother's body to be taken away. The Twins had arrived together without planning to, and right away they conjured a pack of cigarettes and lit each other's smokes, while the Firstborn opened the window. He ran his fingers through his hair, turning his hooked nose in profile, that cartilage that went on growing. He read some terrible jokes from his phone screen without daring to recount them from memory, because one can't count on memory. His jokes followed by the whinny of the Twins. That double, penetrating laughter spread to Ella; not the jokes, but the terrified laughter.

At the foot of the bed they waved goodbye to the Mother, Ella's hand bending at the wrist, the Firstborn's knuckles cracking; the Boy Twin made a victory sign with his fingers, while his imperfect double pointed her camera and pressed record. But the Mother was already surrounded by a wall of stretcher bearers paler than the patient. Her levers were already in motion: they reclined her back, raised the rails, rolled the bed down the narrow hallway, and closed the hatches on the elevator, leaving a vibration in the siblings' eardrums, all four stupefied, sunk into icy orphanhood.

Together they recalled the sinister anecdotes of childhood. The Twins, who hoped to be, when they grew up, a screenwriter (him) and a filmmaker (her), had stored away those scenes for a future film in which a mother tried to murder her children.

The Lady claimed that the Mother had wanted to kill them when they were little. She made them eat potato peels covered in dirt without the Father's knowledge. And she sent the Twins out to play with the stinky kids from the neighborhood so they would catch their bugs. The Lady said these things while she wiped her nose, blew into a handkerchief, let out a couple quick sneezes, but the Girl Twin was aware of the blast wave of hatred that sustained the Lady, that old woman whom the Girl Twin adored no matter how much she detested the Mother and the house she'd chosen for them all, so full of cold windows that let in the dust, so plagued with corners. But the Girl Twin didn't resent that her Mother had made her open her mouth and stick out her slimy tongue to kiss her Boy Twin and the other children of the neighborhood. She rolled with laughter when she remembered it, laughed with her entire face, wrinkling her round cheeks, because she knew everything the Lady said was true, except that the Mother wanted them dead. The Boy Twin seconded his Girl Twin without paying too much attention, and he kept a wise eye on his older half sister, who resented the superiority of her younger siblings. And the Firstborn threw wood on the fire by reminding them that the Mother had almost managed to kill them once. Really kill them. It's true! the Twins sparked in unison, while the Firstborn, pushing the wall with his palms to stretch his calves, went over the experimental treatment the Mother had subjected them to. She wanted to cure your allergies, remember? and he bent his leg backward to extend the thigh. The Twins watched the past play out before them like a movie in the present continuous: those weeks when the Mother injected them with *dust grass oriental planes live cockroaches*, an injection of spring and trade winds. Every Thursday she increased the dosage to make them more resistant. And the Girl Twin thanked her for the needle and then got onto her iron roller skates, tightened the straps around her sneakers, and went down the street on four wheels, but she came right back, skateless, breathless, scratching frenziedly at her red and blotchy skin. She found the Boy Twin struggling against asphyxia *blue violet vomit of stars* in their parents' bed, with the Mother beside him filling a syringe to inject them, first him and then her, with a vial of steroids. The one the Father kept in a cardboard box in the closet, for emergencies.

What cures in one dose can kill in another, the contrite Mother confirmed. There were no more injections, but the Mother didn't give up.

She extracted a pink tablet from her pillbox, the one she kept in her nightstand. The Boy Twin, his eyes shining with allergies, let the Mother deposit it on his thick, rough tongue, and he closed his mouth while the tablet passed the threshold of his uvula and slid down his pharynx. The Girl Twin, with another pink tablet between her fingers, came out with, mom, how do you know this isn't one of your menopause hormones? Quick, the Mother yanked it from her hand to read the minuscule letters on the tablet. The Boy Twin looked at them disconcertedly and stuck some swift fingers down his esophagus, and his retching rescued the pill, slippery with saliva. The three of them stared at it: it was the breast cancer hormone.

In its origin the word pharmacy had contradictory meanings: it was *remedy poison sacrificial lamb*. But there was a secret alliance between these meanings: the sacrifice of the lamb to the gods was destined to resolve problems, poison could serve the community as solution or consolation.

* * *

Didn't aspirin protect against breast cancer? It was strange he hadn't given aspirin to the Mother, but the Father wasn't about to recommend to his second wife the pills that may have killed his first.

The medicine that can save your life can also kill you.

* * *

Which of the two was older was not determined by the secret order in which they were fertilized or birthed, but rather by an equation of the spaces they had lived in, Ella told them, raising one eyebrow and leaving it up in the smirk of a riddle. On a snowy mountaintop time passes faster than in the sea, she said, and even faster than inside the earth, three microseconds per kilometer per year, continued their sister, exaggerating her mathematical superiority, adding that time stretched out at the gravitational center. But we've always lived in this same city and done everything together, objected the Boy Twin. We haven't even gone skiing in the mountains, agreed the Girl Twin, stretching her lip to keep her vanilla ice cream from dripping.

The Girl Twin licked her lips as she managed to destroy her older sister's evil calculations. The Boy Twin, on the other hand, started retching at the smell of vanilla and milk, which reminded him of his tonsils. He didn't remember going into surgery or spilling bile and blood after the operation, he remembered only that they gave him nothing to eat for days but that repugnant ice cream.

The ancients believed that memories were stored in the tonsils, never anticipating that the doctors of the future would proceed to remove those pieces of the lymphatic system, useless as they were.

* * *

Those Twins were hers, hers, no one else's. Ella, on the other hand, belonged only partially to her because she had to compete with the Father, and as for the older son, she didn't lay a finger on him, preferring to leave him, bitter as he was, to her old husband.

They must have had a pleasant childhood, the Twins, mere spectators of other people's drama. They had each other to protect them from their older siblings.

Because Ella used to tell them they were adopted and the Twins, though they didn't know what adoption was, would bawl their eyes out.

Because the Firstborn told them, once they realized they were not adopted, that they'd been cloned. By then the Twins had stopped crying.

Because the Father, trying to convince them to shave their heads, warned them that if they refused, their brains would be fried. The Mother never forgave him for that, but the Father rolled with laughter remembering them shaving each other's head, ending up bald as fetuses. The Twins laughed violently as they recalled that scene.

* * *

The Twins didn't remember that Ella used to cut off locks of their hair so close to the scalp that sometimes she left them bleeding, and the Mother never understood those wounds, those twin sobs.

The Mother concluded that they yanked out each other's hair.

* * *

And something else, whispered the Mother, lowering her voice until it was almost inaudible. What is it? asked Ella, blowing on her eyes to keep her from crying. I think your dad has another family. Another family, thought Ella, looking with *horror fright trembling synapse*, another family? feeling her blood congeal in her chest, her blood pressure drop, but her Father already had not one but two families, the children born of the first mother and the Twins born of the second. Could there be even more families, more wives of her Father, more daughters who were her sisters? she wondered, and Ella thought that if anyone would know it would have to be the Lady, and then she thought maybe the Lady *was* that other woman, a secret mother. Another family? That's what I think, said the Mother, nodding, lowering her voice so much that Ella had to lean closer to her mouth, and the woman must be very expensive, she whispered, he must have a lot of children with her, she went on, and she dried her eyes with her sleeve and wiped her nose. Are you sure? Ella said, pulling the Mother's hands from her face so she could look her in the eyes. I asked him for money for the silicone breast and he told me he didn't have a cent in the bank, nothing, no retirement. How can he not have anything when he's spent his whole life working like a dog? And what did he do with all the money your mother left you? The Mother stared at her and Ella couldn't tell whether her eyes held compassion or accusation, and she felt her blood spin like it was in a centrifuge and her face turn red and then the Mother twisted her lips and dug a hard knuckle into Ella's sternum: you know something.

* * *

His oldest daughter was so thin. The Father made her eat cheese. That extraordinary fat would improve her appearance, and to convince her the Father used the word scurvy, which Ella had just learned. That horrible illness afflicting malnourished sailors. But that cheese contained filth Ella was not immune to and it made her seriously ill, and the Father abandoned his fattening strategy.

The Father gave her a stuffed dog that she named gastroenteritis.

The Firstborn kidnapped the dog and made it disappear.

The Mother found it buried in the yard, years later, when she was digging a hole to plant petunias. Gastroenteritis was decomposed, a defeated dog.

Ella wrapped him up and gave him to the Twins for their birthday.

The Twins kept the stuffed dog's cadaver and used it, years later, for a short film dedicated to the Father.

* * *

Someone had told Ella that the children of doctors ignored their own illnesses, and that doctor parents didn't pay enough attention when their children got sick. Ella had complained of fatigue but *nobody no one not carnivorous plants* had noticed. She complained of tiredness, her head hurt, and it was a coworker who mentioned how pale she was. Could she be anemic? The analysis gave figures that shot up and sank down over the page. You had a virus, announced her Father over the phone when he looked at the report she sent him, and he congratulated her because she'd endured a bout of mononucleosis on her feet.

I don't feel good, the Girl Twin had said long before. It'll pass, predicted the Boy Twin. But the Girl Twin said again that she wasn't her usual self. Once more her complaint fell through the cracks of the dinner table conversation, and there it remained until the Mother found the Girl Twin thinner, sunk into a chair with her shoulders fallen, scratching desperately at her face and neck. You're going to hurt your face, said the Mother, catching her hand and staring into her eyes. Let me see, stand next to your brother? But the Girl Twin didn't get up and instead the Boy Twin brought his ruddy cheeks closer to her, and the Mother saw that the Girl Twin was turning yellow. She was thirteen years old and had severe hepatitis.

But that hepatitis episode was condensed in her memory. All she retains with certainty of that week is the comatose sleep and an intensive convalescence of movies.

Sick from abandonment, the Boy Twin got into bed with his sister who was stunned by fever. Sick from boredom, he turned on the TV that was already in color by then, and he looked for classics that they both watched with deep, empty eyes, ready to be filled by cinema. And since his sister took her time in recovering and the movies started to repeat, the Boy Twin headed off to the video store to get more, each one stranger than the one before, or that's how it seemed to the Girl Twin, who, as she started to get better, began to pay real attention. In those days, in that bed, they decided

116

that someday they would make their own movies with an unused camera that was lying around.

* * *

The Girl Twin had no appetite and lost several kilos in bed. Her Mother got wise, took advantage of her lost weight to warn that if she went back to eating like before, she could suffer a sudden and fatal relapse. The Girl Twin went on losing weight so she wouldn't get sick again, and she was down to skin and bones when the Father, who didn't understand why she was still on a diet, explained that she was immune to the virus. She would never again suffer from hepatitis.

* * *

Before the invention of the anesthesia they must be injecting now into the Mother, doctors had to possess physical and mental strength to operate on patients who were convulsing with pain. But all four of them agreed that the Mother wasn't going to need anesthesia; it was an old joke of theirs, that the Mother went at full throttle until her motor was turned off, that the Mother had only two settings. On, said the Girl Twin. Off, said her brother, and he opened his eyes wide when the Girl Twin said on, while the Girl Twin closed hers when her brother sang out off. They laughed convulsively, hiccuping.

The cold echo of their laughter.

* * *

If it was true that Ella separated the fine skin of the Mother's eyelids to be sure she was still in there. If she was afraid of not finding her, or of finding someone else in there. The surgeon was now opening a different skin with his scalpel, and would be cutting tissue in search of, what? An asteroid, or some meanness of her husband, or burned bread, the excessive radiation of summer, her aversion to the Firstborn? Where did the tangles of the Mother end and her tumor begin? Those were the questions Ella asked herself while she listened to the strident laughter of her siblings, who didn't seem to be asking any.

* * *

In the center of the milky way there was an enormous hole. The breast of an ancient goddess had spilled its milk.

* * *

Speculation about a mutilated breast. There was no anticipating whether they would remove it entirely or just take the glands and ganglia, or whether the sentinel node was already corrupt, whether they could salvage the nipple. The microscope would deliver its uncompromising verdict while the breast waited *open purple palpitating* on the table. The surgeon would issue the final word with his gloved hands, cut.

What bothered Ella was the question of where it would end up, that thing she felt belonged to her even though it didn't. She wanted them to hand the entire breast over to her and not tell the legitimate heirs. She would keep it refrigerated in a jar that she wouldn't need to label.

Someday that breast would be the only thing left of her idea of mother: the forgetfulness of some lips that never sucked at the nipple. Because Ella never even caressed the outside of the body she'd lived inside when she was a bunch of reproducing cells.

* * *

In her time in obstetrics the Mother witnessed the birth of a baby girl who was so premature, so half-made, so *silent contracted cyanotic in the face* that they gave her up for dead. In those days, the Mother said, we didn't know about hormones that patch up lungs or close hearts still separated in half. They threw her into the trash. Don't look like that, the Mother said shrilly when she saw the horror in the Twins' eyes. They had stopped chewing, their forks hanging in the air, imagining that newborn cadaver tangled up with orange peels and squeezed-out tea bags and roast chicken skin. Of course it wasn't a trash can of food, it was hospital waste. Bloody bandages. Umbilical cords. Placentas like purple jellyfish. Well, that's *much* better, said the Boy Twin ironically, and the Girl Twin laughed but immediately hushed. Doesn't sound very hospitable, that hospital waste, observed the Firstborn, going along with his younger siblings, while the Mother said, would you let me finish?

The stillborn girl erupted into a desolate cry and they had to rescue her from her improvised cemetery.

* * *

After several tries, the freckled neighbor across from Ella got pregnant with three eggs fertilized on a glass plate. One of the embryos stopped dividing and was declared deceased, the other two were born prematurely. The boy weighed eight hundred grams, the girl weighed half that and was only partially developed.

The girl will survive but the boy won't, predicted the Mother when her daughter told her about that early birth. Girls survive more because women are genetically prepared to hold up and programmed to survive. Our job is to spread genes across the planet, preserve the species. The Mother always found a way to put one message inside another. Women saved humanity while men made it their

119

job to lay waste, Ella thought, planning to write again and tell her about the baby girl, who really did survive.

The boy died of a brain hemorrhage that was unexpected by everyone except the Mother, who'd seen it coming.

* * *

The premature baby girl didn't have the strength to suck and the neighbor pumped milk and fed it to her from a bottle. She was in the middle of that task when her visitors rang the doorbell. She opened the door pleased to see them, tell them all about the drama of incubators and the joy of seeing her daughter growing, nourished by her mother's body. Triumphant, she brandished the bottle full of her milk, and she lifted her shirt and there was her naked breast, covered in freckles, the wrinkled areola, some thin tubes stuck to the skin, a bag of freshly pumped milk held to her clavicle. Ella looked at El looking at the radiant neighbor's mechanical breast. She saw him go pale.

Don't do that to me again, Electrode, he said to her later. He must have thought she'd planned that macabre show.

* * *

Her Father had been nursed for years because new brothers and sisters kept being born with whom to take turns at the maternal breast; he just got in line to wait until the others were finished. The Firstborn had been privileged with the milk of an ephemeral mother, and the Twins with that of another, long-lasting Mother. But Ella had only witnessed the mammary ceremony of the younger siblings, with aversion, with resentment. Each one sucking at a dilated nipple, both of them dozing at the breast but holding on tight so it wouldn't escape them. Afterward they would burp, sated, lying against that *warm transparent stretch-marked* skin.

My mother's milk was the best, said the Firstborn, as if he were the deceased's only child. It was sweet, he told her. And then he'd be silent and watch what Ella did, but Ella did nothing but hate him in silence, knowing that if she responded he would hit her. Sweet. It was sweet. A wound opened up in her stomach that kept her from moving, *sticks and stones will break my bones*. It would be a long time before she realized that her brother couldn't remember their mother's milk. Sweet. Bitter. Its taste.

But what could Ella know when her orphan mouth had tasted only the bottles that the Lady had given her? Her teeth had already grown in by the time the Father remarried and the new Mother started to nurse the Twins.

Those flesh-and-cartilage siblings, those restless babies who demanded the breast every hour. Those creatures whom Ella made cry.

* * *

Rambling around her diffuse memory are the sisters from that red corner house known as 'the scream.' A house that rose up in a chimney steaming from the cold during the winters of the past in dictatorship. The girls never talked about the father they saw only inside a television, singing to a giant microphone. That father who would later leave the country and die of cirrhosis of the liver. The sisters and their neighbors would learn of his passing through the press. But there they were, the two of them; they'd arrive together at Ella's house, agree to sit in the living cum waiting room, and they would take turns going into the darkened bedroom and removing the articles of clothing that covered the symptom they had just invented, for that day, to be treated. The sock over the broken ankle. The scarf for the sore throat. The opened shirt undressing the asthma attack. Ella was always the doctor, and the sisters from the red house were always patients who let themselves be touched by her practiced hands.

The Firstborn was watching them through the opening in the curtains. He watched as the neighbor took off her schoolgirl shirt. He watched as Ella slid her fingers, curled into a stethoscope down the neighbor's back, and with the same five fingertips listened to the patient's heart as she simulated a cough. Then it was her ear that listened, her cheek pressed against the navel. Then her lips on the nipple calmed that cough-racked chest.

She's not your mom. There's no more mommy. The Firstborn was barking at her with his face inflamed, and he snarled and showed his teeth. Did you forget you killed her?

Did you forget?

She would never forget it, even once she was no longer capable of remembering.

* * *

The sisters stopped coming over when their breasts filled out. They'd been told in school that no one should touch them there.

* * *

The pregnant Mother was confined to bed rest when she got a call from the school asking if the family was going through a crisis. A crisis, repeated the Mother, confused and indignant, how dare this teacher make such an insidious accusation? The grade school teacher cleared her throat while she came up with some way to apologize and explain that her daughter was distracted in the classroom, downcast, pallid. She hadn't touched her lunch or her juice and she'd sat alone at recess with a book she never opened. She hadn't smiled even when the teacher put a little silver star in her notebook, the kind the girl collected because when she grew up she was going to be an astronaut. She had a single line drawn between her eyebrows, and she dragged her backpack. Might her parents perhaps be divorcing?

The Father sat down at the table with Ella and a biology manual. He showed her the illustrations of a hale and hearty ovum surrounded by puny little sperm cells, undulating and sky-blue; one of them was bluer than the rest and had a long head like a comet, and it got ahead of the others and made its way into the egg. There were no *pollen fleshy springtime flowers* anywhere. The next page showed an embryo and the Father explained that the cells divided swiftly until they became *fetuses babies wretched people*, and he also told her that the Twins were two different embryos, double the cells that the Mother could tolerate. That's why she was nauseated. That's why she was in bed. Because any organism would try to expel cells that were unfamiliar, and there were a lot of unfamiliar cells here. He didn't say destroy and he didn't say eliminate, but expel was another of those verbs and the Father couldn't leave it out of his story because that would have been a lie. It was because of those hyperactive cells that the Mother vomited in taxis and had contractions when it wasn't the right time or place, and bled a little in her underpants, but it would be only for a few days, he said, just a few, he repeated, seeing that instead of paying attention to him, Ella was scrutinizing that two-headed monster with her lips pressed into a line. But Ella was listening, and she understood that the Mother would end up making those foreign bodies hers.

123

Error 401. The mandate of multiplication in cells brought cancer as often as children. Confused cells disobeying a prohibition.

＊＊

Amalgam of *nuclear energy kisses on the mouth*, the Twins attracted without repelling each other. A supernatural force kept them united, and if someone managed to separate them, they screeched until they turned blue.

＊＊

How much weight that corpulent woman had gained with the Twins inside, and how fast she'd lost it while she nursed them. In spite of the bread with avocado and the calcium and iron and the liters of vitamin-enhanced milk, the bags of oranges, the bowls of pasta with beans, the *humitas* sprinkled with sugar.

She never gained back those kilos she hated. The Twins wrung out of me all the fat of the pregnancy plus four more dress sizes, the Mother boasted to her girlfriends, sipping a cup of black tea, eating a water cracker, watching them, the other women, devour enormous *lúcuma* pastries with a sheen of grease on their lips.

＊＊

The scant Mother that was left to them was off in some brightly lit room, opened wide, and here, behind closed doors, were her children and another woman's. And because the sun hit them square in the face they closed the curtains and stayed in shadow. Ella noticed that the Twins, leaning against the wall and discussing a movie that had just come out, had become asymmetrical: the Girl Twin round, the Boy Twin rectangular. The long Firstborn was sunk into the screen following the news of the polemical trip of the

Olympic torch around the world, while Ella, a dotted line in the family geometry, wondered about the Father's absence. Various aunts and friends were arriving, the now-widowed Cousin and her five daughters. Bearing fanta and greasy pizza, empanadas with *pebre*, and other products that were forbidden in hospitals. Bearing anecdotes that sped up the time. Reeking of perfume as they came in and out and in.

Ella hugged that close Cousin she had rescued from the waves years before, offered condolences for her husband. The Cousin nodded, unmoved; she had accepted his death, and his memory was already dissipating. What had not left her was the possibility that when he crashed into the truck stopped on the highway in the early morning mist, intoxication flowing through his veins, her husband had remained conscious and tipsy a few minutes longer, alive, alive, knowing he was going to die.

The phone call in the middle of the night woke her up amid *deep-sea currents blind raccoons on the curb*. The policeman's voice giving her the accident report.

The Cousin was the same age her mother had been when she was widowed.

Ella didn't remember having been a little girl in the house of that aunt of hers, a little girl entering the living room, skates in hand and her Cousin following, a little girl hearing her uncle say that he'd spent days with an intermittent colitis and decades with an interminable debt his wife had cosigned for.

They were ruined, but they got by with help from the family.

The Cousin spent vacations with them, weekends—especially with the Firstborn—birthdays, parties, one funeral after another.

Ages later, holding a cigarette between deformed fingers, advancing on feet made clumsy by rheumatoid arthritis, bearing up under her seventy years and an impossible job, the Cousin's widowed mother would tell Ella that her son-in-law's death had hurt her more than her sister's and more, much more, than that of her own husband. It had revived in her only daughter the certainty of a lifelong bankruptcy she would never recover from. As if they hadn't had enough, now the debt would be repeated for her daughter and her five granddaughters.

*　*　*

The elevator opened and out came a man pushing a woman in a wheelchair. In the muscular man, Ella swore she recognized the gym teacher who for years had trained for marathons with the Firstborn. He looked just like that guy who'd let Ella kiss him and didn't tell her brother. He had a wandering eye now, but it was him. Hello. Hello. They kissed on the cheek, surprised to see each other, they hugged as if they'd never stopped caring. The man knew Ella had left the country, but Ella knew much more about him because she'd always wanted to know. She'd known when his girlfriend had a stroke while they were jogging in a park. And later she'd known when he'd had a stroke, too, leaving that eye now uncoordinated in his face, even though he didn't smoke or drink and he went right on training for the races that the Firstborn had abandoned. She was hearing him ask what she was doing in that hospital and listening to him say that his own mother had just had a section of colon cut out.

Their mothers' cancers had reunited them.

*　*　*

Ella wanted to know if El's mother had ever had cancer, but El's mother had always been a healthy woman. Impossible, Ella replied angrily, she must have died of something.

* * *

It hadn't spread through the lymphatic system, the oncologist reassured them, giving them the only smile in his repertoire. The word metastasis could be thrown out as fast as he'd discarded, by dint of *bitter scissors needles inclement sutures*, that cancer. That hard-shell crab, that soft onco. That part wasn't said by the surgeon but rather the Father, who came through the door taking off his mask to give them the operational details, the etymology of the illness.

As if he were clarifying the confused notions of medical treatises, the Father presented the theory of the ancients: they believed that cancer is produced by an imbalance of fluids that, instead of circulating, crystallize inside the body and sink *feet pinchers root networks* into it.

* * *

A scientist had tried to prove cancer wasn't contagious by feeding removed tumors to street dogs. The mutts salivated in anticipation, howled as they waited for those human cancers that were their only food. The drool dripped from their snouts. If he injected them with cancerous cells, would they contract cancer or would their canine immunity protect them? That was the scientist's next question.

* * *

Into the trash went the tattered crab and the whole maternal breast.

The tumor's location hadn't allowed them to preserve the breast, but what to call the process of this loss. Amputation recalled the treatment of a wounded soldier. Mutilation, one who's been tortured by enemies. The Mother had been mutilated, and now they were waiting for the living wound to become a dead scar.

* * *

Still under anesthesia, she touched her chest, and when she felt nothing but thick gauze she howled that the nurses had stolen her breast.

* * *

Traveling mammary story. The silicone breast that the Father had brought into the country during the years of dictatorship. That breast was too large for the aunt of the colleague who had housed the Father during a conference in his discipline. Maybe someone could use it back there, in the past, suggested the foreign colleague, and he gave it to the Father in a square box, in a suitcase that was opened when he reached customs. What've you got there? an official asked him, and he escorted the Father off into a small room— her Father, the degenerate.

They held him at customs under suspicion of importing pornography, or something worse.

The Boy Twin was going to use that scene in the script he still hadn't started to write. The movie of the murderous mother that the Girl Twin would someday direct.

* * *

The Mother is awake, getting to know her wound. What did I do to deserve this? she says, and the older daughter looks up. This, says the Mother, as if she had to explain, losing it all. Is it punishment? she wonders, doubt stuck to her voice. The back of her hand perforated with a needle, the dripping, intermittent IV. You've done so many things, says the daughter, sighing without taking her eyes from the gravitational waves she is finishing calculating on the screen. But not all are so bad, she adds, closing her computer and staring at the foot sticking out of the sheets. A toenail ingrown into the Mother.

Of course it wasn't divine punishment, Ella thought, applying the Mother's frugal of course and the Father's dry tone. People were dying like flies from cancer. Every decade the number of patients doubled, and Ella was sure it was because of the increasing atmospheric radiation.

* * *

A bible on the Mother's bedside table. Without asking, Ella took it to her room and opened it: that antiquated smell brought up memories that couldn't be hers, but arose in her head as her own. Well into the winter evening the Mother came to turn off her light, and, seeing Ella behind the covers of her lost bible, she was pleased. The bible was a big medical tome.

In its pages she learned of the seclusion of patients who suffered from that *deep whitish coarse* tumor that was leprosy. And she read the word pestilence and the word abomination. And she read that nudity was prohibited between family members, and Ella had seen the Twins naked and she'd dried them with a towel. Sin. She'd kissed her Cousin on the mouth to receive her germs, and her Friend, too, in desperate times. She'd showered naked with her Father. And her Father had sinned with that distant cousin whom he later married and had his first two children with. That mother who birthed her was, then, also her abominable cousin, and the impenitent Father would be struck down with lightning, but when? struck down when? she wondered, and when was Jehovah going to give them a thrashing, when would he burn them all with his brimstone?

And what could it mean that in the beginning there was only the word and the word became flesh? She abandoned the medical treatise under her bed and never returned it to the Mother.

* * *

Retching and vomiting that awakened her suspicions. She took a urine test, but her fears were unfounded and only a single line appeared: negative. That same night she dreamed she was on an elevator full of passengers who shook pink pom-poms every time Ella spoke. Every time Ella moved her head. She knew, as one knows only in dreams, that those pom-poms meant she was pregnant. She went back to the pharmacy and the bathroom and urinated on the stick that gave a positive in two red, broken lines.

A doctor who was shorter than Ella confirmed the result, showing her a pale embryo on the screen. It was a *seed bean distant planet* floating in darkness, surrounded by a white web. Stuck to the side of her uterus was where Ella saw it, and she wanted to cut out her eyes. Cut off her face. Cut and run.

* * *

Some of the ancients were convinced that the uterus was a mobile organ whose uncertain orbit produced unbearable pain and fits of madness. What they didn't understand was why a uterus settled into place during pregnancy.

* * *

She'd seen the doctor of the *stray asteroid seed* from a distance when she'd gone through this with her Friend. Because his practice was forbidden in the country of the past, he changed offices every year, moving to new houses more and more frequently, this doctor.

It was an autumn of chronic rain. It was pouring, and her Friend had yet to arrive. The nurses were turning off the lights until none remained on, not even the one in the flooded garden they pushed her out into. Let her wait there, in the dark, while the scornful nurses returned to their lives.

It was raining like in the bible, she thought, and immediately discarded that maternal idea.

* * *

Her Father would go around turning off lights in the house so as not to waste electricity. It wasn't necessary, all that yellowed light, all the white light that altered the circadian rhythms of the species. Seventy percent of mammals had a purely nocturnal existence. But Ella wasn't one of those mammals, not on that black, wet night when she waited for her Friend to pick her up.

* * *

Portrait of a photon, the indivisible light molecule. How were photons calculated in the starry milky way? she thought, but she saw no stars in that water-covered sky.

* * *

The Friend took her hand and led her through streets so covered in leaves you couldn't see the flooded gutters. She opened an umbrella that the wind made sure to twist up, break, drag off into the night, and the Friend cursed the storm that had stolen her umbrella. She opened the door, folded Ella in two to fit into her car, her apartment, some dry clothes, and into her own bed. She injected her with a vial of antibiotics because who knows what kind of conditions that doctor operated in? She lay down beside Ella. Caressed her ear until Ella slept.

Ella hadn't thought again about that bitter, stormy evening.

* * *

The body doesn't lie, but perhaps that isn't true. It's the image that doesn't lie. But that wasn't true either: the Mother's cancer undetected by x-rays was irrefutable proof. And chemotherapy was diffused throughout her body because those cells were fertile, fierce, and invisible as they searched for the organ where they would multiply.

Back in the country of the present, she calls the Mother after each chemo session. The poisoned Mother doesn't remember those calls, or doesn't remember what they discussed. She tells the same story every time.

Every time, she talks about how she has a tube inserted into her sternum so all that poison they'll keep pouring into her won't make the veins of her arms explode.

Whenever someone tells me they're going in for chemotherapy, I feel a terrible sadness, says the Mother, every time.

* * *

Anyone can forget and then remember, but Ella has a memory that eliminates everything: 410 error.

* * *

And she never stops asking what it is that Ella is writing. I know it's not a novel, stammers the Mother, overcome by confusion. No, it's not a novel, I'm not a writer, confirms the impatient daughter. It's a dissertation. A dissertation, repeats the Mother. It doesn't have a plot, the daughter continues, it's full of holes, and I don't know when I'm going to finish, because I haven't even started. I'm just now choosing a subject, and her voice wavers in panic as she speaks those words. Maybe there'll be a chapter on radiation, and she knows she's lying but she emphasizes the radioactivity in case that word resounds and remains in the Mother's dazed brain. I don't know if I want to read it, replies the Mother, sinking down again into her chemical nap. Every time.

* * *

The Firstborn had already left home, but the other three remembered the plague of rats that only the Mother could manage to eradicate. The Mother, who in her laboratory years had worked with little rats so white it hurt to look at them. She put them in her pockets and let them climb up to her shoulder, making the Grandmother go faint when she saw the red rat eyes, the nose peeking out from her daughter's pocket.

Those rats were raw material for all lab experiments because their genes were 90 percent human. And there were so many, though no one knew the number: some calculated an average of four rats per person in the world, but the urban legends ventured eight or nine per human. The only certainty was that a female could birth up to two thousand babies a year.

Her house of the past had housed rats in legendary proportions.

Hundreds of tiny claws darting across the attic: no one could sleep. How were they going to exterminate the creatures? was the question all three of them asked at breakfast, before heading off sleepy-eyed to school. If they found one in the toilet and flushed, the rat went down the pipes and swam back. If they threw one off the roof, it survived unscathed. And it wasn't a matter of giving them just any old poison, said the Mother, shifting a bite of bread to one side of her mouth. They're very smart, she said as she swallowed, they send the oldest or the sickest to try what I put out for them and they wait a few days to see if the envoy survives. If he does, the others dig into what's left.

The rotten-egg stench had already alerted them that one rodent had indeed been sacrificed by the others, which scurried away into holes in the kitchen, leaving trails of shit and terror.

The Mother found a delayed-action rat poison that managed to trick them; for a time the frenetic racing of *tails claws speeding tetrapods* in the attic slowed, and the stench grew.

In the alleyways of her country, in the stadiums and in houses that didn't belong to Ella or to anyone she knew, another fetid breeze was blowing. The Friend, who in those years of the past, like Ella, wore a blue jumper down to her knees and a frayed tie and who sat with Ella at a wooden desk, had told her about the sidewalks where human cadavers had been left, and no one dared remove them.

Those dead people had been labeled as rats.

But live rats were what the soldiers stuck between *legs vaginas screams* of the female prisoners before killing them.

* * *

A poison that was infallible because it was irresistible. One with sex appeal, announced the Mother, without going into detail. She went up some stairs, opened the hatch to the attic, and pushed in some gray balls, then washed her hands with soap and a lot of water to get rid of the smell that excited the rats, which scurried around until dawn, possessed by an orgasmic death.

The rats above succumbed to the Mother below, leaving that horrible smell as collateral. What a rotten stench, exclaimed the Lady when she walked through the front door with each hand holding a Twin's, letting go of them to cover her nose. No, no, said the Mother, watching the little ones put their arms around each other and run into the house. There's no smell, she said. She was smoking cigarettes to cover one smell with another; she ashed her third and blew out a smoke that the Lady cursed. It can't smell bad, she said, because the beauty of that poison is that it mummifies the rats, she murmured in a voice that seemed to come not from her but from the smoke that surrounded her. It leaves them dried out, just skin and bones.

Necrotize was the verb that described that perfect ending. It's not so bad to die that way, murmured the Father. No one's going to want to eat them. We, on the other hand, are worm meat.

The Father had asked to be cremated when his gray matter faded to black. He would stay at home, his presence turned to dust inside an urn, and maybe if she sifted the Father's ashes, Ella could still rescue fragments of his fingernails.

* * *

The singeing rays of radiotherapy were filling her mouth with sores and scorching her skin. It wasn't so long between when they stopped burning sinner women to a crisp at the stake to save their souls and when they started applying radiotherapy to save their bodies. The radioactive pyre went on burning them alive, or furnished them with a slow death that became evident only decades later.

* * *

Her hair falls out all at once in the shower, frayed water clogs up the drain, swirling with shampoo suds and the Mother's tears.

The Lady hears her cries and comes into the bathroom without knocking, feeling sorry for her boss, who sobs as she stares down at her aborted hair. With fright. With grief. Naked even of her eyebrows and dripping wet, the Mother embraces that Lady, who has never accepted her, caresses the mat of *thick unshakeable blue black night* hair just like the locks she's lost.

She had worked in the house even before the Mother appeared, and she went on exercising her wavering loyalty, as if the Mother had a magnetic power that the Lady, rage and all, couldn't resist.

The Lady had gathered up all that black hair and thrown it into the garbage. Then she'd fished it back out again, rinsed and dried it, because Ella, who never called her, had phoned to request it. It's going to smell bad, insisted the Lady, who just couldn't understand what Ella wanted it for, when she wasn't even the Mother's daughter. Or do you plan to sell it for a wig? Ella didn't want to answer, because she knew the Lady was going to say the same thing as always, in her nasal voice. *Niña cochina*. Dirty girl.

Ella begged her to save it between sheets of newspaper until she returned to the past, and she added, her voice thin, please don't ask me any questions.

* * *

The Boy Twin had told them about the time he saw her talking on the phone with the wig on, or on top of her grown-out hair, a little disheveled; something didn't fit and he kept watching her until he realized, thanks to that nasally voice, that it was the Lady disguised as the cancerous Mother, flirting with the mirror.

* * *

Those aunts of hers, the ones who would die before reaching old age, had very thick body hair and they got rid of it with a candle flame. They passed the flame quickly along the skin so as not to burn themselves, and the hair would crisp, the ash would fall in a pile on the floor. Ella gathered it up along with the wax drippings and saved it for future experiments.

Her classmates removed their hair with wax. It wasn't good to shave armpits or legs because then the hair grew back thicker, longer. To see if that was true, she started with her eyelashes. She cut them with scissors and put them all into a jar; she looked at them up close, so trifling. She hadn't thought about how, without eyelashes, her eyes would fill up with dust. That she'd be left with stumps lined up along the eyelid, and every time she rubbed her eyes that edge would scrape her corneas.

They would grow back, longer. And she would burn the midnight oil without batting a lash, all night long. Because for Ella, night was nothing more than the electrical extension of the day. Because Ella had made the night her subject of study.

* * *

She's not sure how old she was that time she got separated from the Mother and lost her in a big store full of *women sweaters scarves spindles*. She saw her from a distance, from behind, and ran toward her, took her by the hand, hung from her warm fingers, feeling her long nails, her ring. Ambient music. Her enormous coat of blue wool and her hairdo stiff with spray. All that jet-black hair turned and showed her the surprised face of a woman who was not the Mother. What an odd little girl, thought the stranger, watching her disappear into the crowd.

* * *

The forms she filled out in doctors' offices in the country of the present certified that Ella was a lifetime member of a cancerous breed. Drastic cancers of the colon, pancreas, melanomas on her genealogical tree.

The godmother, pregnant with her own death, couldn't zip her pants. Absorbed in her cigarette, blowing smoke with a trace of a cough, looking at herself all swollen, she'd cried out, they won't button, and I'm so skinny! The godmother's frail chest, her rickety ribs, her ruined cheeks and that deceptive pregnant belly. They'd given her a benevolent diagnosis but the godmother smiled, cocking her head to one side and squinting her eyes as if she wanted to focus on each one of them, to let everyone know she understood what was going to kill her.

They'd been lying to her mercilessly.

Your boob's out, Ella told her godmother. They were staying in the same room, and from her bed Ella noticed that the godmother's baby-doll nightgown had slipped down. Crowning the breast was a small nipple, like a wart. It's just skin, wrinkled skin with some crazy hairs, observed the godmother, and she winked an eye before returning to her book.

The godmother read in bed, smoked in bed, exhaled through her nose, and let the ashes fall to the floor. The godmother, who as a child had set fire to the palm tree at school to see how it would burn, how fast the flame would ascend, coiling up the bark. The godmother, who passed a lit candle along her legs. The burned smell impregnated the air around that godmother, who demanded to be cremated the day she died.

* * *

And her other aunt had lived more years than predicted by undergoing treatments that couldn't quite halt the reproductive enthusiasm of her cells.

The Father examining his own sister, the eldest, a prematurely old woman. She lay unconscious, plugged into a ventilator that prolonged her last gasps. Saliva curdled in the corners of her mouth. Her head sank forward, toward hands flopped on the sheet as if she'd fallen asleep while praying. The Father pushed that head up by the chin, moved it side to side. He separated her eyelids and shone a flashlight into her pupils, which still contracted. He held the inside of her wrist with his fingertips and counted seconds on his wristwatch, then dropped that arm with its lost pulse.

The eternal bedside doctor: a general hardened by the successive losses of his troops. And although he no longer had a heart, its beating kept him alive. Those three hundred grams of muscle were turning out to be enough to let him see everyone else die.

Why don't they unplug her? Ella asked, hating the artificial life provided by that machine breathing for her aunt. The tenuous swish of her chest was her only movement. And a heart that insisted on beating, that would hesitate for a fraction of a second, would skip one beat and then another before it finally stopped. Those tenuous beats were the only thing that separated her from definitive death, but it was so difficult to die. They'd have to give the aunt something more than the intermittent morphine drip, they'd have to help her. That's a decision I can't make, murmured the Father. And it's illegal in this country to help someone die, even if you don't like it. Ella flinched, thinking that her aunt was already dead.

To whom did it belong, that body that was no longer her aunt? To her uncle, sunk into exhausted sadness. To the uncle who died of a sudden cancer just a few months after his wife.

* * *

Ella is wondering how likely it is that some other surreptitious cell will appear in another maternal organ.

* * *

The Mother will tell her what it's like to choose a wig that matches her hair, to go to bed in her wig, wash it in the shower the way the Father, when he travels, washes his shirts. Wash them while wearing them, scrubbing them with soap like they were his own skin.

Ella has lost track of the future time when she'll open a closet and find the Mother's wig on a white styrofoam head with a blank face. Or the time when she'll closely study the maternal face, the halves of that face framed by black hair and held up by a diminutive body. She'll see herself in the Mother's strong eye and in her fallen one, in the smile of the Mother, who in that faded photo is still the same age as Ella, and she'll think that, though she's not her daughter, they suffer from the same asymmetry.

stardust

between times

He was *tall skinny brittle*. Fragile, like the mother he had lost.

He'd been broken so many times, as if he weren't broken already. Shattered.

And there were so many fissured bones that people lost count or simply stopped counting. Somersaults on roller skates, bicycle accidents. That plunge into the sea after the tide had receded. Cracks during the long training sessions for the marathons the Firstborn ran every year, in spite of the pain in his bones.

To have rolled from a hilltop. To have splintered a clavicle.

* * *

Bone portrait. Living tissue composed of *calcium chalk phosphate stardust* rendered into being on the x-ray plates. That grayish tissue that hardens over the years, gradually goes numb, becomes fragile like an eggshell with its marrow yolk inside.

* * *

The Father's battery had died. His car was an old model, clunky and noisy, and his son was lightweight and taciturn. And although Ella was not strong, she pushed as hard as she could beside the Father while the Firstborn stationed himself beside the driver's window, open so he could turn the steering wheel. The space narrowed between the trees in the driveway and there was a dip in the gravel that the teenage brother didn't know how to navigate: the car, already picking up speed, swerved and hit him. Hit the bone of his hip. The grinding sound of his pelvis as the car crushed his body against the trunk, and her brother collapsed.

The last bone to be named. The one that joined the two halves of the pelvis. The innominate bone. The Father didn't remember anyone ever explaining the origin of that name that refused itself, he could say only that it must have come from the ancients. After *ilium ischium acetabulum sacrum*, they must have run out of steam because they didn't write pubis or coccyx. The Father dragged his finger over the anatomical map and pointed to the exact spot of that latecomer bone the Firstborn had fractured.

In that bit of skeleton: *screws rivets bone graft*.

* * *

If they had taken stock they would have realized that with or without *accidents crashes falls from wobbly ladders*, the number was excessive. It was the Mother who separated the breaks from the accidents that had caused them in order to examine the case. A left wrist, and in the right arm, the radius and ulna. An exposed fracture in the elbow that had to be filled with screws. The rib that was caved in by a training buddy who'd given him a shake that was supposed to fix his back pain, but left him breathless for several weeks. And the clavicle in the fall. And an ankle, the finger shattered in a doorway that the Firstborn didn't even bother to wrap. Four metatarsals of the instep. The calcaneus. The screw in the hip. To have vegetated for months in a bed with a torso in plaster. To have torn the same meniscus twice.

And of course, added the Mother, the front teeth, which were also bones. He knocked them out when he tripped on the sidewalk while fleeing his own malice, turning to look behind him. He'd wanted to escape the shove he'd given his sister, her front tooth that he'd pulled out at the root, but he'd ended up breaking his own, and the other one too. He hadn't put his hands out to break his fall. God punishes but he's not cruel, said the Mother when she reached him. He was lying on the ground, bleeding profusely from the mouth, but he turned his head and shot her a toothless grin. His crow's eyes landed on his stepmother's shoulder and then on the sister who came up behind her, covering her lips with her hands. The resentful glare he shot the two of them then.

He was already punished, the Mother said to herself, glad she didn't have to hit him.

Ella held the tooth in her hand, stared at it in surprise: she'd seen it so many times in the mirror, incisive in the mouth, mounted in the gum, but in her hand it looked like someone else's. She spat out a little more blood and covered the hole with her fingertip.

Among all the sister's crooked teeth, the false one would be the only one aligned with her jaw. Her best tooth the one that wasn't hers.

* * *

She had stashed her front tooth in a little box that later she lost in a move. Or maybe it was the Mother who got rid of box and teeth, just as she did with so many other mementos.

* * *

The celebrated pathologist from a freezing boreal country had realized that bones didn't just grow back together; they also had the ability to lengthen. The pathologist cut *femurs tibias joys* with a saw, taking care not to hew the nerves, then separated them by millimeters, immobilized them with a metallic frame he'd invented himself, inspired by medieval torture instruments, with wires that went through *calluses muscles shrieking screws*. And he waited for the bone to fill in the empty space and forge a longer one. Teeth, on the other hand, didn't grow back or lengthen.

But the Mother had corrected her—some teeth *do* grow. Rats' teeth grew as long as twelve centimeters a year, twelve centimeters of bone that they filed away gnawing at *bricks pipes hard-boiled eggs cement*.

* * *

The Mother never quite loved him, never stopped watching him, because she was secretly afraid of him. The Firstborn had returned from a training session and was hacking angrily at a raw chicken, sprinkling it with a little more coarse salt. His muscular arm resting on nothing.

The suspicion of an anomaly. What if he was doing it on purpose? Doing what, breaking his own bones? asked the Father, astonished at his wife's perverse capacity for speculation. To get attention? So many broken bones just couldn't be normal, insisted the Mother, who tended to fall head over heels in the street and down stairways and would end up sprained or aching but not broken, and who, pregnant with the Twins, had slid in the rain and fallen with her full weight in the entryway of the house, bloodying her knees. Her skeleton didn't have a single break. Her only bony malady was her deformed left bunion.

But the Father dismissed his wife's suggestion. The strange thing was never to break at all, and he didn't want to hear any more about the Firstborn having a problem, not with his bones or his mind.

Drop it, he insisted, and he was categorical. I'm not going to ask you again.

Staying quiet wasn't going to keep her from going over and over the Firstborn's osseous enigma. She frowned and narrowed her eyes, wondering if those brittle bones could derive from the cross of genes between the Father and the distant cousin who was the real mother and also something like an aunt of his oldest children. Such inbreeding brought disorders. Retardation. Bad tempers. Violence. The genetic fragility of bones.

Bad genes. That was the Mother's ruling when Ella told her about the boy who had asked her out. Not looking up from the wall outlet she was taking apart, stripping three copper wires, the Mother rejected him.

* * *

In her memory Ella saw the little Twins unplugging an old transformer between the two of them, and she saw them, seconds later, holding hands while they passed the current from one to the other.

* * *

Except for that tooth, Ella had no experience with broken bones. She didn't know how to interpret what had happened to her foot when she slid on the ice one morning in the city of the present. That quiver when she put weight on her foot to stand up, that limp. The slow trip to the doctor's office where they asked her to lie down on a metal table and covered her with a lead blanket. She hid her hands under it to protect them from radiation. Everyone does that, the technician said with a mocking smile as she took Ella's hands and moved them to the sides. The important thing is to protect the soft tissues.

And Ella had to admit that the technician, whose face was eaten by acne, was right: even she knew that. And she knew that people in a different age had fallen prey to the sensual spell of their own bones and those of others: to see them so defined, luminous, stripped of their skin. Those who could pay for radiographs had them made and exchanged them as gifts and displayed them in houses. Never anticipating the consequences of their profession, the newly rich portraitists of the interior suffered debilitating burns and died of cancer. Or they merely lost their photographer's eye and their hands. And Ella emphasized the bit about the hands and winked at the technician.

You know a lot about radiation, commented the x-ray expert. Not enough, Ella replied, looking at her fingers that no longer wrote.

* * *

Supposedly, everyone supposed—the Father especially, though perhaps her brother had his suspicions—that Ella was still in the city of the present to finish the doctorate that would launch her into the future in the country of the past.

I was just thinking about you, were you sending me signals? Ella lied when she heard his voice, muffled by the long distance. The

146

Firstborn dodged the question with a curt announcement: he would be coming to visit the following week. She knew he wasn't coming to see her, but rather to run in a marathon over *dead-end streets bridges black tunnels holes* marked with signs in every language of the planet. Did she have a mattress where he could rest his bones for a couple of nights? As many nights as you like, Ella said, fearing the meeting would rekindle the resentment they had always felt toward each other. And although her uncertainty scared her, she set up a spare bed in her shared apartment and put it next to her own.

And she waited for him at the airport and received him with an unexpected hug that the Firstborn accepted rigidly. She wasn't sure what they would do next. How she would talk to that brother of the present with whom she hadn't spoken enough in the past. Her brother had spoken to her only with his hands, with fists.

Together and alone, *eating sleeping snoring laughing aloud*, they had never done that.

They had been parallel universes advancing toward the future.

* * *

Ella could only remember waking up at midnight with the answer to an algebra problem that she hadn't been able to solve during the day. Twenty-four, she thought, or fifty-six, while in the room next door she heard the Firstborn tossing in bed or grinding his teeth. She felt she wasn't alone.

* * *

Tell him about scenes of family life that he had missed when he left for the south; tell him about desiccated rats in the attic so as not to tell him that his departure had been a relief.

Tell her that his years as a southern student had been the worst of his life. The Father wanted him to go but had sent him off without a peso to his name, against the objections of the Mother, who, even suffering that difficult son, would have preferred he stay or receive an allowance. That boy, sullen as he was, wouldn't make friends, and desperation could make him turn to drugs. But the Father had said that wasn't his problem, maybe it would be good for him not to have any help, and when the Mother started to cry he told her that his son didn't deserve it, and neither did he have the money to support him in another city. I know that wasn't true, said the Firstborn, he must have had a lot of money somewhere, the money my mother left him, he said. But I never saw a cent of that inheritance, he said, did he give anything to you? And he threw Ella a malignant glance that she couldn't stand and she lowered her eyes so he wouldn't see her shame. He gave you some money when you came here, didn't he? But Ella shook her head, and with her eyes still on the ground she murmured that she'd received a grant.

In those days, said her brother, I used to study under streetlights so I wouldn't have to pay for electricity. Leaning against the post, he'd gradually doze off until he dropped the book and it woke him up. He was cold a lot, ate very little, almost always fried eggs on bread. Once, while he was heating the oil, the Firstborn turned around to take the last egg from a carton when a rat jumped into the frying pan full of boiling oil. It shrieked, burning, it twisted up, smoking there in front of the Firstborn as he watched it without moving. The little eyes. The tail drooping over the edge of the pan, the oil still crackling. He extinguished the flame, finally, turned around, and ate the egg completely raw.

He threw the frying pan into the trash by its handle, along with the crispy rat, now cold.

* * *

Hadn't the Mother talked about how cunning rodents were? His brittle voice, his cavalier glance. His sister reminded him that every species had its suicides.

* * *

And together they remembered the time Ella came into the kitchen just as he was showing the wound on his knee to the Mother. The Mother had cried out that it was full of pus, but Ella heard a different word, a mistake that she herself had been corrected for so many times. It's not pronounced pus, mom, she said, sharpening her seven-year-old voice. It's *pues*.

Her life was a series of 400 errors impossible to resolve.

* * *

And Ella introduced him to the classmate who lived with her in the apartment that she would leave one year later. The girl was tall and so thin she stuffed socks into her bra to fill it out, and she never smiled but maybe that's why—because the Firstborn didn't know how to smile, either—her brother could take an interest in her bony roommate. The roommate with lips pressed into a line, who typed tirelessly on the computer and scratched with equal fury at her head under a tangle of dreadlocks. She's going to draw blood, observed the Firstborn, who the whole time he was there avoided shaking her hand or leaning back in the living room armchair. He didn't want to catch her lice.

* * *

During those short days of his visit to the present, Ella wanted to take him to a show that he wouldn't find in the city of the past. They took the subway all the way out to the freak show, and there, still, was the contortionist, tall and thin like her brother, the same arms, same scrawny thighs, but with an empty face and clumps of hair so stiff with gel they seemed to defy gravity as they shot out in all directions. The contortionist bent himself backward and stretched out and lassoed himself with his legs and emerged from the knot of his body at the other end and assumed human form once again. He was capable of slithering around a chair and between clotheslines. He put the palm of his hand over a glass, and, forcing it with an elbow, pushed the entire hand in, fingers bent backward. She kept watch over the Firstborn's reactions, looked for signs of *surprise disgust unsustainable complicity*, but her brother had studied this case in his kinesiology classes and the contortionist didn't move him at all. He cared only about athletes injured by muscle contractions, tears, inflammations, or sprains brought on by deteriorating cartilage or breakage. Never outlandish extensions of connective tissue.

The Father predicted that the contortionist would die young. He's too young to die, Ella protested, frustrated and confused by the turn her Father had taken in their phone conversation after the Firstborn had left. What's he going to die of? That contortionist wasn't a virtuoso, said the Father, he was a sick man. He was missing the glue that kept the *organs nerves atoms sewing machines* in working order. Sooner rather than later, his heart was going to break.

That was her Father's specialty: filling out future death certificates.

* * *

For every 1,000 people who die each year worldwide, only 1.9 die from diseases of connective tissue or skeletal or muscular systems, while 17.7 die of diseases of the nervous system. Of the digestive system, nearly 42, of the respiratory system, 53.5, but of the circulatory system, 398.8 die. We know what will cause the death, but not where it will happen.

* * *

Extinction story. The solar system would burn out some five billion human years from now, unless the gravitational force pulled the planets out of their orbits sooner and made them collide. Earth would collide with Mercury or Mars and become an enormous red star where no one could survive. It's unlikely but not impossible, Ella explained to her brother, to prove she understood the logic of the universe.

* * *

I never would have thought you'd want to write a dissertation, you were always so dyslexic, says the Firstborn. I've never been dyslexic, Ella says in her defense, it's just that you were always hounding me, you were always attacking me, you made me stutter, and I was a little distracted but I was always interested in the stars. The Firstborn disguises his rivalry with his sister, saying, sure, but that's not enough for a degree, I just don't see you writing a doctoral thesis. And he was unequivocal in that. She didn't see herself finishing her doctorate either, but she'd tie herself to the chair if she had to. And how is that dissertation going? The Firstborn is insistent. Your Father does nothing but talk about that dissertation no one understands. But no one had asked yet about her progress, no one had asked that question. Not even her Father, who had simply agreed to hand over his savings. She bites her lip while her brother says to her, even in his dreams he talks about your doctorate, as if his life depended on it.

* * *

Ella brought him the pot overflowing with pasta that he had to finish that night, before the marathon. He ate slowly, as though tasting each and every noodle, until he let out a big sigh and she realized that in a few hours they would fire the starter's pistol and she would see him take off, slip through the runners without a sign to her, without looking back, without a thought of her. She imagined his centrifuged head rising up above the others, his tangled hair mussed by the wind, the number stamped on his chest. He'd turned out so tall and slippery, she thought, and she went on thinking about the hole her brother would leave in her as he disappeared into the crowd.

The wind rose up *cirrus cumulus atmospheric variation*. The river, black with oil, traversed by sewer rats. And in the noise of striding steps, of running shoes and laces thrashing the cement, of panting and booming voices and applause, Ella would hear the echo of his question.

Did you forget?

How to forget her older brother's punishment at the slightest provocation. How he'd trip her. The front tooth that never recovered. The *pushes shoves low blows*, the bruises stamped on parts of her body where the Father couldn't see.

She let her brother hit her as if each blow could cure a prior wound.

***

There he was, on the spare cot, keeping her company with his snoring.

Her brother's analog and mortal body kept company with another, digital body that couldn't manage to redeem him from himself. He'd holed up in the apps on his phone. One measured his breathing and told him how well he had slept, another marked the race route, counted his steps, and told him his split times, the average temperature of his body, his pulse rate, his blood pressure. He put in earphones while he did his strength training and splintered off from the world and from himself, because he trusted only those devices. Ella wanted to send him a conciliatory message, but her phone transcribed it in the wrong language: *Ahí jopo yo slip well, hay labio.*

The phone did the same thing that Ella did when she'd tried to sing, in the past, songs that seemed written in the languages of other planets.

* * *

Did you forget?

She could hear the past repeating like an echo. She heard her brother calling her a murderer or a mom-urderer but didn't understand what he meant or why her Father told him to shut up. Why the Firstborn defied the Father and kept throwing at Ella that dart of mother and of death, murderer, mother-murderer. Why the Father had lost his head that time, why he'd grabbed the Firstborn by the elbow and put him in a chokehold that dislocated his shoulder and shut his mouth once and for all.

The Father lost his head every now and then. That time in the elevator when he almost left Ella without an arm.

What floor did we live on then? asked Ella. On the sixth, I think, writes the Mother, who after some months in the old apartment and already pregnant with twins made them move to a spacious and shady house she could feel was hers alone. The apartment was number 628, adds the Father, who would never forget where he lived with his cousin, his long-gone dead wife.

* * *

Ella still dreams of being in elevators. A recurring nightmare: the mechanism gets stuck and from inside, from deep inside, through transparent doors, she sees people talking or listening to music on headphones while they wait to go up. They don't see Ella pounding the walls inside, calling for help.

Different dreams, same time period. The dream of the elevator that can't go up or down but slides around in the hollow insides of the walls, the whole length of the floor, and shoots out the side of the building. Ella is saved from a fall by waking up. The dream of the elevator that rises, gaining speed, and breaks through the ceiling of a skyscraper like a spaceship resisting gravity. The dream of being unable to enter the elevator because it's blocked by a woman who's fallen across the doorway, *fat naked shit-smeared*.

* * *

Her Friend, who at the time was doing her psychiatric rotation, suggested that perhaps she was dreaming of her dead mother. You never miss a chance to remind me of her, Ella replied, dipping her fingers into her glass of wine and flicking it at her Friend's face. Just like my brother, what a nightmare.

* * *

It had been a strange case, dying in the delivery room. Even in a dictatorship that sort of death was rare. Women gave birth in the most adverse circumstances, but they died of other kinds of violence.

One women out of every twenty died in labor, said the Mother under her breath, and the daughter was convinced she had made her mother part of that statistic.

* * *

The Friend was sure that under the dictatorship, if an imprisoned mother died, her newborn was secretly given to another family.

* * *

The Father had come back from the hospital carrying his newborn daughter. He gave her to the Lady, who covered her mouth with her hand as she pressed that malnourished baby to her breast.

And she remained there behind him, the Lady, like a howl. The Father walked to the table and sat down and leaned on his elbows and murmured something under his breath, under his teeth, and then he went mute, as though he'd already said everything he had to say to his son. He never mentioned her again, wrapped her in folds of his *brain guts oblivion*.

The son could never forgive him for that, either. His mother's absence was an organ that went on secreting anguish within his body.

* * *

It was the Lady who explained to him why his mommy hadn't come back from the hospital. The boy didn't want to know anything and he wanted to know everything, but the coldness of those words slashed at him. And then the Lady tried to console him, but the boy was fast and he slipped away from her embrace.

To hug another woman was a form of betrayal.

* * *

Almost nine, that's how old the Firstborn was when he lost the mother who for him would always be the only one. He would come to love the replacement a little, but he would never call her mom.

Love her before. Love her after. Love her now and never love her again, not then. Because then was always the wrong time. Never the time for love.

* * *

The Firstborn blamed Ella for having aborted his mama in labor, for having adopted that other woman. But that other woman was more Mother to Ella than the body that had contained her until she was dispatched into the world.

* * *

To remind him of the blows, once, at that bar. The Firstborn shielded himself behind his glass of wine, and he asked, with a tongue weighed down by the past, was I such a rat? He composed a stingy smile in which Ella saw her brother's resentment, his rage, his unresolved jealousy. You were very much a rat, many rats, Ella replied, feeling her voice become poisoned, because her brother had taken his revenge out on her for too many years. Rats lived only twenty-one months, if no one took the trouble to kill them sooner, but her brother was still alive.

He remained a difficult brother, and she still had a bone to pick with him.

He seemed untroubled, but Ella noticed the slight flare of his nostrils, the twitch of his eyelid, a carrion bird crossing his conscience.

* * *

Years later, every time El brandished a shoe in her face, Ella would think of her rat of a brother. She'd swear to herself she would turn El in if he ever touched her, not realizing there was no need for it to come to blows before she left him.

It was her brother who had left home, and that had saved her.

* * *

He didn't want to watch TV, was his excuse for not sticking around. Had he stayed, he would have changed the channel to avoid seeing the Father recommend aspirin to the entire country. The Father's unbearable assurance, in his house, in his office, on the TV screen, the little box of aspirin in his hand.

The Firstborn took only dipyrone, and only when the atmospheric pressure changed. Because his bones hurt. Because his bones held up columns of air heavy as lead, his bones full of marrow. He would never take those other painkillers that liquified the blood. Because it was excessive blood that had killed his mother.

He ate little and quickly and finished before his siblings, got up from the table with his empty plate. The family paid him no mind, gaping as they were at the black-and-white screen that showed telenovelas instead of political news. And he left his plate in the kitchen and went out the front door and through the gate, leaving it swinging in the wind, and without stretching first or warming up he hurtled out into the street and ran the kilometric avenues to the park and then up the precipitous hill. And if he wasn't drained by then he'd sneak over the back road and climb with his hands over earth and skinny trees, yanking on bark, weeds, thorns, until at the top he'd reach a slender plaster virgin with arms outstretched and head bent, granting forgiveness to someone unknown. He scorned her kindly farce, he spat on the edge of her dress before starting his descent, letting the wind dig its needles into him, covered in *mud fleas suicide bees* and scratches, her brother bit by a spider, covered in old scabs.

Her brother, trained by resentment, was preparing for adulthood.

He gradually ground down his knees, undid his joints. He always returned to the same house, the same table with the same black-and-white TV that they would punch to wake up, only to set off again on his supersonic escape.

Her brother the rat, running on his wheel, believing he was moving forward in his cage.

So as not to be in the living room with all the traitors and strangers who considered him part of their family, the Firstborn got a broken-down bicycle and spent hour upon hour out in the city, and when that wasn't enough, he pedaled to the lake on the outskirts where he learned to swim.

To swim against the current, never with it.

* * *

All of them gathered and waiting for the Father to appear on the screen, a fleeting star. A smile across Ella's face. The Twins with their spoons full of mashed potatoes, open-mouthed, engrossed. The Mother saying, kids, please swallow, your food is going to get cold.

The imposter Mother trying to erase the memory of the real one.

* * *

This child has pinworms, the Mother would say, before saying, later, when he started to break, that he had porcelain bones. The porcelain boy, the Mother called him when the Father couldn't hear. The cracked boy, and she'd lower her voice so the Firstborn couldn't hear, though there was no danger of that, he was already too far away.

He was getting rid of the rust in his joints with every turn of the pedals and every stroke of his arms. That's what he said, that it was rust, and other times he said he was oiling his joints.

To run wanting to catch up with the mother who'd left him behind. To suffer muscles hardened by lactic acid. To know that the painful substance, lactate, was also found in mother's milk.

* * *

Ella waited for him at the finish line, and when she saw him dragging his foot she suggested he sit down on a nearby curb, where they watched the last marathon runners arrive, trotting, tripping, walking. The Firstborn smelled of sweaty earth and cement; he smelled like a stranger. Like someone who no longer needed anyone, someone who could do without.

And yet he had to lean on Ella when he stood up. The air pressure had changed, that's why he couldn't walk. That's what he said. Don't be silly, Ella murmured, stopping a taxi.

* * *

What was he going to study, medicine? The Firstborn's fork froze over the chard casserole, and he replied that he detested that profession of charlatans. They gave names to everything they couldn't cure. And he looked sidelong at his Father, who was silent, bruised by the words. The Father destroyed by the son. The Mother swallowed her food as if her mouth were filled with dirt. No one killed her. No one let her die. When are you going to understand that? Everyone dies the best they can. The Mother knew that wasn't true, but she turned her white-hot eyes to him and saw the son's face darken above his incipient beard and beneath his striking brows. His cranial bones vibrated. His chest rose and fell from hyperventilation. He was swollen with oxygen. He was going to explode. He put his palms on the tablecloth, one, two, half a second, rose abruptly to his feet, launching the chair backward, and he went out *running running running running running* as if fleeing a plague.

That house was the depository of all that would never be his. It was inhabited by the impostor and by his traitor of a sister and other children who were only his half siblings. That house was not the small sixth-floor apartment where he'd had his only mother.

* * *

It was during that time when he got into extreme sports. When he broke the rest of his bones. When they feared for his life.

Someone has to die for a sport to be considered extreme, El noted. If your brother had died it would have been according to his own rules. Stop, Ella said, cutting him off. Can't you see his corpse would have fallen onto my shoulders?

* * *

Even though it's snowing, the birds chirp at the top of their lungs. Even though it's nighttime, the light, white and brilliant as it reflects on the snow, confuses them, and they don't know what time it is. That's what she tells the Firstborn, and then she tells him more.

The tower rebuilt after the attack that brought it down had powerful beams pointing up to the sky, illuminating the route of so many lost souls. Those rays interrupted the migratory routes of birds, and thousands of them got tangled up in the light, whirling around *drugged hallucinating interrogated by bright spotlights,* noisily flapping their arrhythmic wings. Trapped in the light, they finally fell from the air at dawn.

Birds with failing hearts exploding on the pavement.

* * *

Speculation about the bone callus. She'd imagined that the Firstborn's skeleton must be covered in hard scars, but El explains that those calluses are scabs that gradually disappear as the bone recovers its shape. That's why past fractures aren't easy to detect against a backlight. But if there are no traces, why do bones hurt? Her brother groans in pain when a storm is coming and creaks when the sun comes out. He's become an expert at predicting even the slightest variations in atmospheric pressure.

How're the bones? El would ask over the phone every time Ella called her older brother, the last Sunday of the month. She made sure El was home, she insisted he say hi to her brother and ask about his skeleton. Ella, always trying to mend the fracture of childhood.

* * *

They were eating empanadas downtown in the preterit city, beside the museum where they held the annual human rights conference that El was attending. What are the worst bones? asked the Firstborn, separating the pit from the olive. El didn't need to think about it, his answer delayed only by a sip of beer. The ones eaten away by sulfuric acid.

That's what El would talk about that afternoon, about people who didn't die *beaten broken suffocated insomniac earth*, but rather disintegrated in industrial-strength acid.

* * *

You remember that filthy stream at your grandma's house? Ella was opening curtains. The one we washed figs in? Or more like got them dirtier? We were acquiring immunity, answered the Friend's medicated voice, her ragged voice, so many years later. Her ailing face, her lipstick smeared just like her grandmother's, whose face Ella could still see, the dust from the road stuck to her cheekbones. And remember when your grandmother caught us throwing eggs in the middle of the dictatorship, you remember?

It was necessary for the Friend to remember those times, and to forget others.

And maybe it was better not to remind the Friend now about the larch tree stump where she'd taught Ella the theory of the concentric circles that would let them calculate the tree's age. In the trunk's rings you could read the changes in the earth during its growth, the Friend had said in her high-pitched little girl's voice. Periods of drought, years of sunshine. She'd planted her finger on the circle closest to the bark. This is where my parents disappeared, she said very seriously, and then fell silent, her nail digging into that line. That, she added defiantly, your stars don't record. We named them, but it didn't do any good. Ella hadn't known what to say then, but looking at her Friend now, slumped on the sofa, those same fingers longer now, that skinny hand scored by veins, she wanted to rescue her from the dictatorship that was coming back to destroy her; she wanted to shake out her clothes, open the blinds, and wipe off the glass with the end of her sleeve; she wanted to point toward the stars they had once stared up at and shared. Because it was true that some stars had already been extinguished, that their light was merely phantom. Ella would have liked to tell her to accept that her parents now belonged to the past, that the two of them also belonged to the past, that there would be a time when someone looked at them from the future and thought they, too, were still there. They would be the mirage. But telling her that would not help quiet her Friend's neurons, sparking in midcrisis.

She was recovering from a completely atemporal nervous breakdown.

She'd just received their bones, her parents' bones had just been found.

* * *

Every Friday the Cousin stayed over to sleep in Ella's bed while Ella, who hadn't spoken to her since the day she rescued her from the waves, who didn't want to see her again, who had stashed her bathing suit and her jars of sand and shells in her closet, went to spend the night in her Friend's starry yard.

* * *

The Cousin and the Firstborn fastened the four wheels to their sneakers and crossed the avenues on skates without brakes. They launched themselves from the top of a paved street. Holding hands, the two of them, rolling downhill with their arms outstretched; they were algorithmic birds flying high that Saturday when they spotted earth and rocks stretched across the street where the hill ended. Scattered in the mud they could see sharp pebbles, but at that speed it was impossible to stop.

Lying on the street she swallowed dirt and spat out her cousin's name, too scared to look and see what condition he was in. She stood up slowly, feeling her arm was rotated at an unlikely angle, and when she looked at it she saw, through her torn sleeve, that a stone was embedded in it. And she tried to take it out but she couldn't, because it wasn't a rock but the tip of her broken bone, the *dorsal radius ulna* poking through her skin.

To be unable to identify one's own bones.

Only the radius was broken. The Firstborn thought of his bicycle braking before a fall, of *dislocated axes gears punctured tires*, of the impossibility of escape. Ella thought, listening to her Father describe that wounded arm, of the radial velocity of the stars.

***

They intervened in the Cousin's arm with *plates screws nuts washers*, and they sewed her up and put her in a cast. But the plaster was too tight and her hand gradually lost feeling. That haughty Cousin who chewed her nails and the skin around them, bit until she drew blood, pulled off the scabs without feeling it and she kept on going until she bit something very hard in her fingertip.

Portrait of an amputated bone of which nothing was left to be said.

***

Some people suffered disorders of the nervous system that inhibited the experience of pain. As if they were blind or deaf to touch, those people cut or burned themselves and stopped only when they saw the damage, or smelled it. Those people died young, declared the Father. Pain exists for a reason, after all.

To die young, murmured the Father, who was old by now and still alive. Young was what his first wife was when she died.

The strange thing was that the Firstborn had averted so many tools of death. Power switches and loose cords. Windows and their balconies. Too-clean glass. Rugs where feet went sliding. Ladders and stairs. Belts around the neck. Ropes. Pipes. Knives, spoons, toothpicks sunk into the throat. Toothbrushes buried in the jugular. Stray bullets. Loaded guns. Shrapnel. Fire. Unbreathable smoke. Odorless gas. Plastic bags on the head and pillows over the face. Cleaning products consumed too enthusiastically. Poison. Insecticide. Recluse spiders. Snakes full of venom. Rabid dogs. Walls shaken by the earth and fragile cornices that plummet without warning. Branches that fall without warning. Planes that crash, without warning. Trains derailed. Slippery ice. Wet streets, curved avenues, highways without shoulders, and enormous and minuscule cars. Trucks turned off, stopped in the fog. Bicycles careening in the wrong direction. Speed bumps. Zebra crossings. Yield signs. Stop signs no one respects. Traffic lights on red or yellow. Choppy ocean waves. Flooded or empty pools. Faulty genes. Germs of all kinds doing what they do. Sleeping pills. Overdoses. Allergies. Attacks of asthma, or sadness.

The Cousin was pleased as punch with all that iron screwed to her arm, unaware of how much titanium the Firstborn carried around.

* * *

The Father scolded him for putting the Cousin's life at risk. What was he thinking? The same thing you were thinking with my mother, replied the oldest son, taking refuge in his plaster armor.

Father and son cracked their knuckles in silence. What they could have said with words they told each other in osseous code.

Someday, in the future, they'd get to the marrow of the matter.

* * *

165

The afternoon was already dissolving over the beach when the Firstborn climbed up some rough rocks, balanced one on top of another, to dive into the sea. Below him swelled the tall, clean waves, almost free of foam, but the tide was already starting to recede, those waves were withdrawing, and it seemed like the water itself had shrunk, that the ocean had gone dry and all that remained was the wasteland of rocky sand and mollusks stuck to the ocean floor, seaweed, fish *flailing incisive salt-suffocated gills*, and starfish alive and dead moving surreptitiously over that nothing on which the Firstborn, flipping into the air and stretching out on the wind, fossilized now from fear, was about to break his head.

The lifeguard saw him from a distance and then close up, body to body. He arrived kicking up sand with his heels but someone had already called the ambulance. They laid the Firstborn on the sand and asked his name, and he had a hard time remembering.

It was a summer of curfews, and the Father, who hadn't heard from his Firstborn in some time and was many kilometers away, received an urgent call, and he said, yes, yes, he's my oldest son, lowering his voice until it was inaudible, where is he, where did you take him, and without asking if his son was alive he grabbed the car keys and said, let's go, let's go, get your coat, and the Mother put on a wool cardigan covered in pills and missing a button and they sped off toward the coast. They drove without asking any questions, or maybe just one very brief question: TBI? Just three letters and a question mark because there was nothing more to say, TBI, but it wasn't TBI but a closed-head TBI, closed and dark as the sky of that night now almost closed—soon they wouldn't be allowed on the highways without running a big risk. The Father didn't think about the hour or the restriction but about that closed head, swollen, bleeding inside, and he accelerated between hills and slopes and sharp curves, no *moon light at the end of the tunnel*, no cars going in the opposite direction, much less people. They saw nothing but the mutt that leaped into the road and looked at them with red eyes and froze in the high beams for the hard blow that killed it. Because the Father, instead of turning or braking, accelerated over its body, resolved not to look in the rearview mirror.

When he pulled up to the hospital and turned off the engine and got out of the car and woke up the stiffened nerves in his back, he heard his wife say that the front bumper had fallen off when he hit the dog. That's what it's there for, replied the Father without turning around, hurrying toward the emergency room.

* * *

Instead of closing up in a neat line, the Cousin's wounds widened and scarred over. They gave her an elastic sleeve with metal plates to squash the scabs that were never going to disappear.

The keloid had been described by the ancients, but it was the moderns who gave it a cancerous name, close to cancroid, which called up something that the keloid was not. Because it wasn't cancer or a tumor even though its thickness was due to the frenetic reproduction of cells. The Cousin had always been prone to those lesions: her *fiber skin scab fear* overflowed the limits of the original wound.

The Cousin didn't believe that all wounds needed to scar over or that all scars were ugly, even if they were thick, rough, hard. She was going to make hers part of her allure. When others saw her bare arm and wanted to know what had happened, the Cousin declared, without getting upset, that her mother had stabbed her with a knife. Or that she'd been carried off by a kite that landed her in a picture window. Or that she'd been bitten by a rabid dog, and they'd had to shoot it to make it let go of her. Once, she said she'd been attacked by sharks in the same choppy sea where once she really had almost drowned.

* * *

El told the Firstborn a story about his dentist. He knows my job is identifying bones, and he gave me this riddle: How do you tell if someone was alive or dead when they fell from a building? Then he ordered me not to close my mouth, and his thumb pressed the crown into my gum and he stuck his hand in my mouth all the way to the back of my throat. And, El went on, rather than think about the body falling alive or dead, I thought about that awful habit of asking questions when the patient can't reply. The dentist gave a dramatic pause as if I didn't know the answer, El said, while the Firstborn pressed his lips together and extended a finger to draw a question mark in the air. And El assured him that any forensic scientist could answer that question. If the wrists were broken in the fall it means the person was alive. We all put our hands out when we fall, by instinct. Only if we're dead do we not try to catch ourselves.

The Firstborn smiled uncertainly. He never put out his hands—he tried to catch himself with his elbows. Years before, they'd put one back together for him with stainless steel *plates nails barbed wire*.

* * *

In that fall with the Cousin, the Firstborn had dislocated his elbow and fractured his shoulder. And although it was forbidden, he went out to jog under the full weight of his plaster torso.

* * *

Portrait of an elbow. Instrumental joint. Hinge of the arm. Loose-skinned bend. Of the whole skin suit, it's the corner that is most wrinkled, most aged, most tattooed by falls. Its strangeness was that it bent backward while the rest of the body pointed forward.

168

Men think because they have hands, claimed the ancient poets. More recently, other thinkers suggested that men, but not women, move because they need something. It was a version of a saying that the Father had once uttered: necessity creates the organ.

The Twins didn't walk, didn't stand up, didn't show the slightest bit of enthusiasm for crawling; they spent their days lying on their backs staring attentively at their two pairs of feet, the cinematic proliferation of their toes. Concerned, the Mother asked the neurologist at her hospital to examine them. Their only problem is laziness, her colleague concluded, taking off his horn-rimmed glasses and combing a hand through his gray hair. Make them.

The one who took care of making them crawl, stand up, and start walking was the Firstborn. He bribed them with sweets.

* * *

The Firstborn told El that he could empathize with the anguish caused by the disappearances because he felt his loss was similar. But you know what happened to your mom's body, you know where she's buried, you can visit her, replied El, realizing as he was talking that Ella had never mentioned where her mother was, and maybe neither of them knew. The Firstborn turned pale.

Grim, skinny as a rail, he got on his bike and sped off, taking a detour on his route downtown to head toward the cemetery. It had taken him years to get there, and now he took hurried steps between centenary pantheons and mausoleums and niches dotted with desiccated flowers, mums, until in a bend of the path he found the grave that held his mother. Her full name carved into the stone disconcerted him, the two dates indicating the insufficient years she'd survived to live, the age she'd never reached. He calculated the years his mother had been rotting alone under the stone, the *centuries worms winter winds* rising up with the mother, her cells mixed in with the filth of the city. And all those white chrysanthemums whose scent blended into the cemetery's intoxicating floral smell—where had they come from? There were so many, and they looked so fresh. He wiped the sweat from his forehead. In the distance, a caretaker with rolled-up pants and canvas sandals was watering clumps of carnations. Irises, lilies, weeds embedded in the granite stones. The Firstborn approached without a greeting, without looking the old man in the face; he cracked his knuckles one by one while he got up the nerve to ask, in a deathly voice, whether the man might know who had left those flowers in the crystal vases, the ones at the third grave from the right. The caretaker counted the headstones and nodded. Oh, yeah, sure I do, that old gal, as if the Firstborn knew who this gal who came to see his mother was. And, struggling to open his hands cracked by the sun, the caretaker described a short, thin woman whose sweetish perfume hung in the air every time she went by. She must be the deceased's sister, said the old man, still holding on to the hose, and he added that she came every month, that she got down off her high heels and knelt beside the grave to place her chrysanthemums or her thornless roses, some enormous bouquets, always white. And she made the sign of the cross and prayed awhile. He raised a pair of seasoned eyes marked by deep crow's-feet, and, lowering his voice, confided that a while back the old gal had skipped a few visits. The poor woman was really sick, he said, pointing to his head; she wears a wig now. Real good people she is, he murmured, thoughtful or sleepy, his rigid finger still against his forehead. She always leaves me a tip for taking care of her departed.

The old gal, the Firstborn repeats confusedly. He's on his bike with his hands stiff on the handlebars, his bones covered in *muscles tendons gloves sorrow*. The old gal. The high heels. The tips. The wig. The Firstborn comes to a red light but instead of stopping he pedals faster between the cars and he curses himself, because he understands that in all these years the only person to visit his mother has been the Mother.

* * *

For days he had the rarefied smell of flowers planted in his nose, the buzz of bees in his ears, and in his eyes, the caretaker's cracked hands. Those hands that couldn't open. He should have told him that in some places of the world, bee venom is rubbed on stiff joints and beeswax on worn skin, but instead he was struck dumb.

* * *

Bees have lots of eyes, said the little Twins when the Firstborn went to pick them up at school. They have two big eyes and six little ones, babbled the Boy Twin, and his sister put three fingers on her temples, eyes, three of them here, and they circled him, buzzing around him, telling him he was a flower and doubling up with laughter.

* * *

His face was that of his genetic mother but only the closest relatives knew that, plus the Father and the Lady, and none of them ever mentioned it. And the Mother who came after had made her portraits disappear, all the pictures where the first wife posed alone or with the husband she would leave a widow. There was no image left of the mother holding her son by the hand or in her arms, smiling. Not one. The Firstborn couldn't bring himself to ask her what she'd done with those photos.

Her voice hoarser than ever, the Lady swore to the Firstborn that the Mother had placed other photos on top of them, in the same frames. Polaroids of the fat Twins on her lap, the teenage sister with an illegible diploma in her hands, the Firstborn with his eyes glued to the paving stones. But his *mamita* was still there, watching them grow up, peering through the holes of other eyes. The Lady wrinkled in an exaggerated smile, and the Firstborn asked if she thought he was stupid. He'd already taken the frames apart, and his mother wasn't there. The Lady pressed her lips together and nodded and went to her room, to her drawers, to a shoebox, from which she retrieved the only photo she'd managed to save.

He lingered over the profile of his dead mother. The high topknot of her era. The earring that hung from her ear. He ran his finger over the hooked nose that made him more masculine while it made his mother more real.

＊ ＊ ＊

The Firstborn had gone to bed early because he'd be up at dawn for the marathon, and he'd left his wallet beside the camping bed, within reach of Ella, who was still awake. Her hand crept like a tarantula over the rug and reached it, opened it slowly, slid her fingers into the folds full of cards until she found her mother in that single faded photograph on the threshold of two eras. Beside her stood the rejuvenated Father, who was looking sideways at his distant cousin, caressing the shoulder of that mother still a bride who was discovering the camera right at that instant, as though caught by surprise.

The Firstborn suddenly snored, his breathing stopped for a second, and Ella stared at him, startled. She saw her mother in her brother, obliquely, but right away she vanished.

If Ella had inherited that arched nose the Firstborn had gotten, she never would have operated, not a millimeter of *bone cartilage uvula mother*, she would have jealously defended that nose from the

172

Mother, who went through life prescribing that a person slice off anything that might be considered extra. Fat and wrinkles. The hump of the nose her brother treasured and that Ella would have liked for herself.

* * *

In a future scene, the nurse who extracts blood for a routine test palpates Ella's forearm and tells her, you've got good veins. I'm sure you get that from your mother. Because sons inherit their father's afflictions and daughters get their mother's genes. That's what she says, and Ella turns her eyes toward the room's paltry window thinking that she would have liked to *suffer share inherit ruin* her mother's affliction.

Her biological mother had deprived her even of her genes.

Nor did she look like the Father, as some people told her in an attempt to console her.

Every time Ella described an ailment, the volunteer Mother exclaimed, like me at your age. All Ella's aches were those of the other Mother. Those infections, the Mother had had them. The extremities that would fall asleep on Ella in the future had fallen asleep on the Mother in the past. Ella's suffering was nothing but a repetition.

A hundred times the question: Whose carbon copy was Ella?

* * *

Even the Mother had archived the suspicion about the eldest's anomaly, while the Firstborn secretly studied his skeleton and understood that only exercise could make it sturdier, lift weights, pull pulleys, increase the number of push-ups, squats, sit-ups, but now not

173

even his muscles could protect him. He injured himself training and he could no longer run or jog, only limp; his pain was deep, untouchable. He crossed the finish line of his last race dragging a fractured heel and a pinch of shame.

Ella took him to the hospital in a taxi to see a doctor after an eternity of refusals to be seen. The radiologist sent him to the rheumatologist, who sent him to the traumatologist, who confirmed he had spent his whole life suffering from osteoporosis.

Suffering, repeated the Firstborn, going back over all the steps he'd taken, knowing that the pain had never been in his bones.

* * *

All the fractures of all those years fell into place, but instead of asking him about his bones, Ella wanted to give a radiant spin to her brother's gloomy situation, telling him how the earthquake that year had fractured earth's axis, changing the terrestrial incline by eight centimeters and shortening the day. Her brother said nothing, and Ella filled the silence on the line with her enthusiasm. We're spinning faster. The days are now 1.26 microseconds shorter. If we need to in the future, we could force new fractures to incline the orbit even more and avoid collision with some planet or asteroid in free flight.

Her brother cut her off midsentence. Ella filled her lungs with air. Her Father, she was sure, would be interested.

* * *

Porous bones? That's what he has? I can't believe you don't know what osteoporosis is, her Father reproaches her. *Lies galactic invention*. Lies that bore into the bone.

Really? The Mother opens her clairvoyant eyes. But that's a woman's disease! And it's a terrible sight, the gums that appear in her mouth when she separates her lips to add that the Firstborn's mother had broken her hip once or maybe twice. She was my mother, too, Ella corrects her as she listens to the list of breaks the biological mother suffered in life. Now the Mother is saying that it must be, of course, it's a genetic failure inherited from that *mother aunt now-distant cousin* of the Father. You were spared, she intones, but Ella wonders who would want to be spared from their inheritance. Genetics are not always destiny, she thinks.

gravity

* future time *

In her pocket, her fingers again found something hard and sharp, like a tack but curved. It was a clipping of her Father's grooved fingernail, from his hands that were a world. He used to leave such remnants of himself for Ella to find later. If her old Father were to die suddenly, she knew she'd go on finding him in her pockets.

They won't ever rot, the Father said with a certain arrogance. And Ella confirmed that this part of her Father was immortal. Over the years she had stockpiled those paternal filaments in a clear glass jar that bore a label with the Father's name. The fingernails stuck to her damp fingers, then fell heavily to meet the others.

No call for disgust. They're only dead cells. Immortal keratin cells.

* * *

But now her Father was going to need a tricky surgery. Couldn't they wait for her? Ella sent that request as a phone message to the country of the past.

It's a very simple procedure, replied the Mother, months before the operation. He'll be back to his usual routine in a week.

No need to worry, said the Firstborn, assuming a right of primogeniture that she hadn't granted him. He's almost eighty, Ella replied, and I live far away.

Aren't you putting the cart before the horse? suggested the imperturbable Twins, each from their phones in the bedrooms of their apartments. They repeated, each in their own way, each with the same words, what the Mother had said about the simplicity of the procedure.

Can't you wait a month, until my classes are over? Less than a month. Ella had already bought a ticket for a Friday, just twenty-eight days from now. But her Father had taken too long making up his mind and now they couldn't wait.

* * *

He'd always been resistant to interventions from his field. He played down his aches and pains. His occasional diarrhea, his habit of vomiting for no apparent reason. The migraines that laid him out in bed. His tendency was not to submit to any tests, because they always found something, and it was never what they were looking for. That part he liked to say with a victorious smile. He had treated his heartburn through an informal consultation with his colleagues, smoking with them and smoking alone, smoking while he attended his patients, and eating *pigeon wings mayo potatoes merkén*, drinking too many cups of very black coffee to hold up under the exhaustion of his shifts.

Go see a doctor, said the Mother, smoking with him.

One distant early morning of burning or reflux or nausea, the Father got out of bed. Ella, already asleep, didn't hear the weight of his steps on the parquet, but a white light pierced her eyelids to wake her, then she heard the Mother's shriek pounding like a fist on her eardrum. In her memory the fall had slowed, while the Mother's cry lengthened out. And in that lapse she saw the Father's shape collapsing in its full length, crumpling little by little, in slow motion. She saw him now on the threshold outside her room, the Father reaching out his fingers full of nails, digging into the wall in search of a handhold, but all he caught was the useless ridge where the wallpaper overlaps.

The paper torn as he fell and the Father lying across her doorway, blocking it. The tips of his bare feet. The Mother was kneeling beside him and sticking her fist into his mouth, and she ordered the Firstborn to turn him over so he wouldn't asphyxiate on his own vomited blood. Her Father's stomach full of torn fingernails clawing at him from inside.

* * *

The doctor who arrived in the ambulance locked himself in the bedroom with the Father and the Firstborn and the Mother swollen with twins. They sent Ella back to bed, to sleep, as if that were possible.

She'd never suspected her Father knew how to cry. Maybe he was learning, that night. His sobs passing through the wall that separated the bedrooms were a pounding death rattle, or no, they were a choking cough, an intermittent howl that Ella would never hear again.

It could be he was crying because he was going to die. Soon it would be dawn.

* * *

Wait for me, Ella insisted.

There were things she would never forget.

Her Father stirring the stainless steel pot, hours, days, for life. The ignominious pot that boils only for the Father, still on his feet in the kitchen from back then, still young in pajamas that grow over a body thinned by the ulcer. Ella sees him stirring a rice pudding with skim milk, the powdered milk of those years, the usual powdered sugar, the cinnamon sprinkled sparingly. That Father biting the dust. Grains of rice scattered over the counter. Meteors entering the atmosphere, leaving an ashy trail through the kitchen.

He gets through his convalescence staring into that pot. Poached eggs. White noodles. Apples that the Father peels with a fine knife, its blade sharp and rounded. The apple's armor crumpled on the plate.

* * *

The diminutive Mother couldn't hold the Father up when he lost consciousness. And now that he was old, her Father—so given to fainting—could shatter.

If only you'd seen him back when he used to get kidney stones, said the Mother, rolling her eyes. He'd fall on his back. I've never seen such a man. Although it's true that pain is as bad as giving birth, she

180

added, sorry for leaving him on the floor. The Father had birthed little stones through a narrow channel not designed for that labor.

What had become of those calcium seeds? Ella could have asked for them, could have saved them in one of her jars. She could have rolled them over the cement like she'd done in school with her marbles.

A stone the size of an avocado pit, only wrinkled, had been removed from the Grandmother. Ella gazed at the gallstone the Grandmother stored in her perfumed writing desk. She rolled it around in the palm of her hand.

* * *

Nowadays, the students of her preterit country didn't play with marbles. They went out to protest in crowds, carrying posters, speakers on their shoulders, their little brothers and sisters in tow, orphans of authority, dancing, denouncing, spitting, uncontrollable, breaking windows, breaking ranks, hit by *nightsticks tear gas water cannon sulfur* that threw them to the ground if they couldn't get away.

They fell on their backs sometimes, broke their vertebrae or their heads, while the students of her present dozed in their chairs, far from it all. She wondered if they would ever wake up from that apathy.

* * *

The bird that was her Father had few feathers left now to cushion his fall. He owed the only broken bones in his medical history to those fainting spells. A screw installed and removed, a plaster shell, bone calluses now vanished: a record of fragility far surpassed by his Firstborn, now submitting to the calcium injections he'd been prescribed.

* * *

Wait for me, it's only twenty days, Ella asked again on another call.

Her Father was not a sickly man, but a catastrophic one. He's always been like that, or at least as long as I've known him, and that's a long time, said the Mother, twirling a lock of hair around a finger, pulling on it, making sure it was firmly rooted in her head. It was always like that with doctors.

The Mother was remembering that appendix operation when the Father almost bled to death. Strange case. I opened. Cut. Cauterized and left him all sewn up, said the surgeon, who was the Father's friend. An extreme case, but unrepeatable, don't worry, the Mother assured Ella, like a ventriloquist's doll, lowering her voice so the Father wouldn't realize they were talking about him, always behind the true dummy's back.

* * *

They weren't going to wait for her. They hadn't waited for her, either, for funerals or weddings. Graduations. Births and baptisms. She'd learned after the fact of the Twins' premiere at a small art house theater, she'd received the link to the short film and some photos. Ella lived outside of spontaneous family planning. She didn't remember birthdays. She didn't call for saints' days, because she'd come to despise sainthood.

She didn't know the exact day they would wheel her Father into the operating room. The Mother wanted to let the Father tell her the date. Your dad hasn't told you anything about his surgery? The

TV news now background noise. The Father *swallowing cats biting his tongue* beside the phone. When do you plan to tell your daughter? the Mother asked her husband, separating the phone from her ear for a moment.

But the Father wasn't going to talk about his prostate with his daughter, much as she may have existed there, come from there or maybe from a testicle, Ella thought, anatomically unsure but thinking she still had the right to know. Even if the cell Ella had once been bore no resemblance to the person she later became.

* * *

Portrait of a prostate. A dark, fleshy nut covered by a delicate nerve network that controls it. Irregular territory crossed by the urethra that secretes its own liquids, as long as the nut is not swollen and obstructing drainage. If that happens, its hidden location will have to be reached with a cesarean cut.

* * *

One old man asks another how much he'd managed to piss the day before. Could you? Yes, replied the less hunched man, more or less. More or less? asks the first. More less than more, a few drops, says the other. Me too, says the first, it's a miracle. It wasn't a great scene, but it was the only one she remembered from that movie.

Ella had slept with enough men to know that some of them escaped to the bathroom at night. That some of them urinated in the tub so they wouldn't have to flush, or standing, or sitting in the dark, trying to hit the target and leave no trace of the nocturnal piss.

The shoemaker's son is always barefoot, but in the doctors' house silence is bared, and euphemism goes in flip-flops. That Mother who described all body parts in gory detail used an alternative name for those organs situated between the legs: the nether regions. She talked about her own infected lands to evade any fleshly detail. She asked after her daughter's regions, her occasional symptoms. Of sex, back in those days, not a word.

* * *

Ella would never talk to the Mother about the call from that stranger who said he was carrying out a phone survey limited to high school students. That learned teacher's voice informed Ella that the principal of her school had recommended her because she was an outstanding student. Was that true? inquired the voice, and Ella stammered while the voice asked if she would be willing to answer the survey privately. Ella agreed. She closed the door and sat on her bed, because that man's convincing voice instructed her to get comfortable and to tell him if she preferred not to answer any of the questions. That was also part of the study, a fundamental part. OK? She agreed and the voice asked if she was ready, and Ella said she was, and she told him her name, her age, and that, yes, she had seven periods—she loved math, science, and spanish, which one did he mean? and the voice assented, yes, you have science and math but you haven't had a period yet, very good, it was very good, she shouldn't worry about that, the voice added, aware that Ella was getting nervous, and what are you wearing right now? My school uniform, Ella said, and the voice confirmed that her uniform was the perfect clothing, and Ella sighed. With knee or ankle socks? and Ella pulled up her socks, ashamed at the worn-out elastic, and she lied a little, and the voice must have suspected because it immediately repeated that Ella should be comfortable during the survey, comfortable and relaxed for the questions it was going to ask. They were very simple questions, Ella would see. And then the voice wanted to know how many hours a week she spent on homework, wanted to know if her studying left her time to rest,

wanted to know what she did for fun when she was alone, alone
with herself, in her room. That was an essential piece of information, she could tell the truth because the answers were anonymous.
Ella thought for a moment before saying books, she read a lot, her
dad gave her science manuals, science, the voice repeated with disguised surprise, about the body, the sky, Ella clarified, very good,
replied the voice, and at night, Ella went on, she looked at the sky
with the small telescope her godmother had given her. Telescope,
at night, the voice was repeating as if taking note of her responses.
And didn't she ever play? Play? asked Ella, who wasn't so little anymore. Play with yourself, the voice suggested, and it added, as if
dispelling doubts, big people's games. Ella wasn't sure she understood but she didn't dare ask again and the voice murmured in
her ear, didn't she ever touch herself? and Ella felt heat wash over
her face and she said no, a confused no, unsure of what her denial
meant, maybe she'd failed the survey, and the voice went lower as it
told her that she was big now, surely her hand played between her
legs, surely she touched herself like a woman. Ella said she didn't
know. The soft voice, the firm voice, so masculine, warned her that
if she wanted to answer the survey well she'd have to follow its instructions, and Ella agreed because it was going to teach her something and she always wanted to learn. Intrigued, she let the voice
guide her hand over her jumper and her fingers over her thighs and
inside her body *soft warm fire electric pulses* while the deep voice
demanded to know what she was feeling now, and now? while she
moved her fingers, but then Ella felt that a different, hot breath was
coming through the phone and she recognized the Mother's furious
voice ordering them to hang up, calling him a dirty old man, yelling,
I'm going to call the cops on you.

* * *

Years later she would confide in the Mother about the irritation down
there. The Mother ordered her to lie on the bed, open her legs wide,

and push a little so she could examine her with a flashlight. I don't see any yeast. Are you sleeping with someone?

She had the impression the Mother was smelling her.

* * *

In any case, the Father had exiled his children from those regions that were starting to fail him. Over the prostate there always hung the possibility of irreversible damage: incontinence, impotence.

What does he care about impotence? He's had four kids with two women? Ella says, not thinking. The Mother protests, offended, glaring at her. Hey, your dad works quite well, I'll have you know. Ella interrupts her, crying, mom! and pointing to a red light she's about to run.

* * *

Call me as soon as he's out of surgery, Ella says before hanging up. And she sits beside the phone worrying that there goes her family doctor.

And the phone rings: everything went as expected.

And it rings again: there were post-op complications, says the Mother, using that euphemism so full of uncertainty.

She gets another call. The Father is on his way back into surgery. He's lost two liters of *willful excessive nauseating* blood, and he's still losing it. A body doesn't hold all that many liters.

He was sewn up tight, I promise, the Mother implores, her mouth dry. She'd been right there next to the surgeon, masked right there, capped right there, all in green with her small feet slippered, and she'd checked the sutures stitch by stitch and given her approval. It was well sewn, not even air could enter the wound, and then the bandage had sealed it. It wasn't spilling out, it was *filling swelling soaking exploding* inside.

Now they were reviving him with borrowed blood in a slow nocturnal drip. The urine in the bag had returned to yellow, but the next morning the Father was bleeding again. Again they were taking him to surgery. Open and sew. Cauterize any tiny seeping veins. Install another catheter. Staple the skin. The order of events in the post-op disorder.

***

And then the Mother, haggard and olive-colored as her surgeon's uniform, didn't call anymore. The voice on the phone calling from Ella's other country belonged to the Boy Twin, and she demanded explanations from him as if he were her Father's clumsy surgeon. It's no one's fault, replied the Boy Twin without apologizing, because besides the surgeon there were other doctors, there was the Mother— who never missed an operation—and there were advanced technological devices that took over as extensions of the doctor's hands. Ella thought about all of that. And there was anguish in that thought, rage in that thought, the thought of a fatherless abyss. She tried to hold it with her body, but it slipped from her hands. The Father inside Ella, right between her kidneys. She had an attack of contractions, an uncontrollable urge to urinate. She sat on the toilet and pushed, but her regions were dry. They were arid places impossible to leave behind. And so Ella raised her voice and the Boy Twin lowered his so much, so much that suddenly he wasn't there, it was a different voice, the Girl Twin's unmistakable voice that used the same paternal parsimony to repeat that she shouldn't get so upset, everything was under control. Under control? Ella asked, raising her voice an octave. Under control, repeated her younger sister. Everything would turn out well this time. This time? This time. Ella couldn't figure out if the Girl Twin was agreeing with her, or if she was kneading her words into a sticky mass before throwing it back in her face. Shut up, Ella said. You shut up, ruled the Girl Twin, losing patience with her older sister. And stop shouting, I can hear you fine. We're taking care of it, we're here with him, and her vocal cords trembled with rage. We're all here. All but me, the older sister muttered drily, letting out a sigh that sounded like an accusation. And she hung up so as not to wake the neighbors, who must already be awake. El was awake now and standing next to Ella, who was a beaten dog. She wanted to howl.

And the Mother, where was she? She must be washing her blood-spattered hands. She must be sprucing herself up for her imminent widowhood.

***

Ella's hands itch so much. She can't stop rubbing her palms over her pants. El tells her to stop doing that, it makes it worse, Electrocution, they'll only itch more. Ella smiles every time he gives her another electric name, but this time she pushes his hand away. I don't know what else to do, she replies, scratching herself with her nails. I'm not prepared to lose my Father.

He was taking too long to die, thought El.

***

Premonitions of the future in the story her Father used to read her at bedtime. In that story a boy is mourning the loss of his mother, and an elf takes pity on him and gives him the bobbin of time that he can use whenever he wants to avoid *pain penance baaing lambs.*

The elf warns him that he must advance the bobbin only in situations of extreme necessity, and the boy agrees but soon disobeys. It's so easy, so convenient, to flee toward the future when he feels fear or hunger, when he's caught stealing in the market or doesn't want to go to school. He skips over hours, advances days, loses five years at a time, abandons all the unpleasant moments of that life he hasn't experienced as his own: he reaches a premature old age, and there's no thread to pull toward the past.

It wasn't hard to stitch together a moral: you can't play with time, because it isn't flexible and it could break. The future was made of the same material, the same streets and houses, the same people or others like them, the same rotten stench. You shouldn't run from the present, said her Father, the same man who sank into bed between the sheets and disappeared for days so as not to feel what might cause him pain.

Sleep cure was what he called those temporal escapes.

The Father decided to extend his future when the Twins were born. He was an older man with a young woman and those newborn babies whose heads were deformed by a narrow birth canal. They were purple and wet and shrieked furiously because it was humid and cold outside the Mother, because the cord that fed them had been cut and their first taste of the breast left them unsatisfied. But the Father felt as if they were shrieking at him because he was an old father and because he stank like an ashtray, because he chain-smoked, crushing out one cigarette after another. And because he'd spent decades with a cigarette attached to his lips, he wouldn't get to see them grow up. What a bastard of a dad, the Father said to himself. The newborns' eyes opened, their lips separated to bare their gums, they bombarded him with their howls. The regret echoed in his conscience. He had to last for them the way he'd already lasted for his first pair of children.

He poisoned himself with one final pack, and, still dizzy from the nicotine, he set off for his parents' house on the city's outskirts, armed with sedatives he'd gotten without a prescription. And he climbed into the bed that had once been his but that was now too small for him and he took the drug that put him to sleep for eight hours straight, nine long hours in a state of death that returned him to life, and he sat up in bed and swallowed another glass of water, another pill, and he urinated and brushed his teeth and sank again into nine or six nightmare-free hours, which then became seven or ten, because he would need an immense amount of time to destroy his lifelong addiction. He lost kilos during those days and it seemed the bed grew while he shrank, his blood demineralized, muscles without tone, and when he finally lurched to his feet he saw his beard grown out and full of gray, and he shaved. Withdrawal started to set in while he returned to his *time city countless children* and he overcame it by sucking on candy bought in bulk and chewing gum and guzzling drinks sparkling with sugar and bubbles. And the toothpick that replaced the cigarette gouged out the fossilized chewing gum between his teeth. He gained weight while he survived for those Twins, who had now reached the age of twenty-five.

* * *

Ella wakes up with her eyelids swollen, hungover. She reheats the coffee El had poured for her. How much would a ticket for tonight cost? she asks El, and he purses his lips, thinking it will cost a fortune. He starts to investigate, trying in vain to soothe the negative charge Ella is emitting. Ella tamps down her hair and swallows an aspirin dry, rolls up her sleeves, and starts filling the suitcase she would have packed three weeks later. But how much does it cost to change my ticket? she insists from the living room, now finally waking up. It's really expensive, El protests from the room next door, maybe the trip can wait a couple of days, Electra. The nickname doesn't amuse Ella at all right now, but she doesn't have time to complain. Right at that moment she gets a message from the Mother. She attaches a photo of her husband laid out in the bed, his chest sunken, receiving the second, fourth, fifth platelet transfusion. Her husband hazy from so much foreign blood. The thick tubes, the monitors beeping at different frequencies, a whisper of respirators, valves, faint lights, trays, and the thermometer no longer of mercury. The Father motionless, eyes translucent and fading: only his messy hair seems immune to misfortune. When did he stop using gel? Ella wonders, and when did he shave his mustache? And she laughs without knowing why, and she starts to cry, knowing perfectly well why.

And the Mother's comment with the photo: *he's much better today*. Much better than when? Ella thinks. It's not a photo the Mother has sent, it's an unbearable twist of the knife.

* * *

Portrait of a dying man with his watch on the nightstand. What she's looking at is not her Father, but *withered skin flesh cells lost on the floor*.

* * *

She cursed the airline that had asked for a birth certificate and a physician's note to process the change fee discount. She cursed the very polite employee who'd kept her waiting beside the phone since dawn. The taciturn morning sun slowly rose, the murky air cleared, and it was already five in the afternoon when a compassionate, bureaucratic voice called to announce the emergency policy they would apply to her. The airline accepted the documents, much as the handwritten letter was illegible, much as the doctor emphasized, in printed letters, that the patient's situation was merely serious. They'd made her wait nine hours to cancel the change fee, but not the difference in fare, which multiplied the cost of the ticket. Ella restrained herself: she understood that this badly paid airline employee had not written the rules, and she said this with murderous calm. She didn't know what this woman's position in the company was, but this, if you ask me! she added and then stopped, contained herself, palpated the gland that ruled affections, the thymus, beneath her thorax. And she finished by freezing her voice again: This is abuse. I could sue you for this, and she declaimed every letter of the suit. The employee stammered and asked her to hold just a minute on that electromagnetically disturbed line, and before a minute was up she came back to let Ella know she no longer had to pay a thing, that she should leave right away or she'd miss the flight.

Meanwhile, there were incoming texts from the Firstborn offering his miles. His thousands of miles traveled over land and through air. *I don't want your miles*, Ella wrote in capital letters, or at least she would have just a few years before; now, though, they were reconciled. Perhaps she wrote a *thanks* on her phone, a *no need*. Perhaps she thought about telling him to keep his miles, the way she had kept all the money her Father was now going to need.

* * *

She doesn't remember who closed the suitcase. Who called the taxi. Whether they sent a copy of the new ticket to her email address. But there's a KLYMJ knocking about: the reservation code has been etched into her mind like curse words in other languages. What time she got on the plane. Whether there was a delay. Whether she accepted the tray of food, chugged a glass of wine, swallowed a sleeping pill, whether she ever shut her eyes.

Who said what, no idea.

404 error. Data not found, while the Father risked his life in that hospital.

* * *

She finds the corner and is entering a facility she has never set foot in before. She goes through its high gates, leaves behind its uniformed watchmen, reaches the entrance of a shabby gray building that overwhelms her. Only Ella knows why her Father has chosen—why he's had no choice but—to go to that old military hospital she now drags her suitcase through. So bone-weary. So beaten down. Practically no fingernails on her scabby fingers. Pain in her jaw and even her ears, and now she's getting into the elevator, one more nightmare. Instead of white coats, the personnel here go around in khaki clothes and black boots. Military insignias over their chests.

A nurse at the entrance to the intermediate care unit is clipping her nails. Her Father must have planned that strange welcoming committee.

Ella stops to take in air: she hasn't breathed in twenty hours. She can't show a single sign of emotion, or else her Father will think he's worse off than he is. Because there is his hollowed-out face. There he is. He opens his eyelids and struggles to organize a grimace that may or may not be a smile. Half a slipshod smile and the ventilator hiss, his heart beating on a monitor. Into his veins drip lazy liters of saline and iron that supplement the blood transfusions, and there are so many cables and tubes going in and out of his body that her Father seems like a being from another world. An extraterrestrial. The weightless hair his comb is unable to tame. His electric head now subdued. She sees him run his fingers through his silvery hair as if he wanted to scratch his brain.

193

Hija, he murmurs, squeezing the word from his vocal cords, not pleased to see her, wondering if she's come to say goodbye, if that neutral expression masks a premature mourning. Maybe they haven't told him the whole truth, maybe he doesn't want to know.

You're so pale, her Father observes, you look worse than me, you look like death. And he laughs quietly, shaking on the cot, full of mischief.

* * *

Conjecture of anemia. His pale fingernails that take forever to grow. His flaky skin. The deep circles under his eyes. The memorious Father's imprecise memories. And those thoughts that exhaust him, the not knowing, when he wakes up, where he is.

The Father in a hell of bodily relativity.

* * *

So what happened with your arm that was falling asleep? Here it is, wide-awake, Ella says, raising it effortlessly, opening and closing her hand several times as if squeezing out the memory of an electric summer that had conspired against her. But Ella had recovered and she had her whole life ahead of her, while the Father seemed to have only the life behind him. Though maybe he didn't even have that left now.

And how's that country you live in? murmurs the confused Father, unable to remember the country's name, unsure that, whatever the country was called, it had any future beyond falling to pieces. Isn't it time to come home? Come back south before the north is extinguished, Ella thinks, come back before it blows up or the universe falls in on it. Ella wants to tell him that it won't happen anytime soon, the planet still has five billion years left, and they will all be dead long before that ending. But she also thinks that maybe the end of the world *is* at hand, because there are almost no bees or wild animals left, or people with their heads on straight, people who would oppose the atomic threat of *cruel despots immortal leaders* that had to be faced up to.

It wasn't one country or another. It was earth spinning toward its total dissolution.

* * *

No one understood the reason for that spilled blood, but while the Mother tore apart her lunchtime bread—because she was eating nothing but bread—she implied it could be a hematological complication. Circulatory, the daughter paraphrased, but the Mother disagreed as she dragged the bread around the edge of her plate. Something in his blood, some kind of deficiency, she explained. Because it wasn't the first time, remember his appendix operation? How long ago, twenty-five, thirty years, the Twins' age. Ella must have been only eight, but she knew the episode that the Mother had related so many times but still insisted on repeating now: the episode of the competent surgeon who was astonished by the severe hemorrhage of his *colleague friend victim patient* whom he had to resuture. And once was bad luck but twice was a pattern, a clue. The Mother adjusted her glasses on her nose as if they would improve her insight, her clarity as she reviewed the facts, and as she took them off again she declared that it must be a problem with clotting factors.

* * *

Factor 7 or factor 8: that was now the bloodthirsty question.

* * *

Though he's already lost so much blood, the doctors ask for one more test tube. The lab nurse tangles up *hands gloves fingers tourniquet* while she's trying to hit the vein, and when she finally spears it she's hit by a spurt of that weak but living blood that still circulates through the Father's veins. It spatters the nurse's face, and, ignorant of his disease, she starts to spit.

Her Father grunts without letting out a syllable, but Ella knows he is thinking the word *ineffectual bungling incompetent inept*.

∗ ∗ ∗

Convalescence story. Weeks of long anemic naps. But no one rests in hospitals: aides come and go, and the nurses enter with their insomniac, indistinguishable voices. How do you feel, doctor? How was last night? But the night suffers the routines of the day, the night wasn't his refuge, but rather a restless daybreak. The shifts *change grate degrade* the patients. Doctor, your paracetamol. Doctor, your anticoagulant. Doctor, your exercises. The changing of the sheets. The four o'clock snack, doctor. Doctor. Because the doctor is bound to his bed like a common patient, ever available. Because every medicine has its schedule, every check of temperature, blood pressure, sugar, and there are distasteful dishes covered in a fine sheet of plastic, little spoons in sealed bags, trays that someone places before him whether he wants to eat or not, whether he's awake or out cold from the lack of red blood cells.

And with the nurses and aides come the *urologist hematologist anesthesiologist surgeon colleague*; they come in, measure his urine in milliliters before throwing it out and washing the bottle, they compare it with the previous emission, and ask him, again, how do you feel? have you eaten? have you slept?

And the visitors never leave, the uncles and aunts and cousins divvy up the schedule and flaunt their strident voices, oblivious to the place they're in or its rules, no shouting, no eating, no breathing, and the nieces and nephews laugh out loud as they celebrate their reunion after years of not seeing or thinking about one another. The Girl Twin nursing her chubby baby, the Boy Twin annoyed by acid reflux and his sister's brazen breast, and someone knocks at the door, excuse me, may I? and behind the question the Firstborn enters and now they're all there consuming oxygen and saturating the room with malignant CO_2. Peering at the Father, panting and gaunt, they say to one another, he doesn't look so great.

* * *

If he is sleeping, Ella slides that short green curtain along the rod so the pale rays of winter sun don't wake this Father who has chosen a hospital of old, mended sheets, of curtains not long enough to cover the glass. Chosen is a way of putting it, but the Father doesn't have a cent left because of everything he gave to Ella and Ella spent. Whether he leaves the hospital alive depends on Ella. That's why she won't let anyone in. Not even her Father's wife, who has taken that ancient weight from her own shoulders and placed it onto the daughter's, who accepts it as long as the Mother goes to work at her private clinic and leaves them alone, finally. Ella has become his sergeant. The door is the checkpoint that halts the nurses who always wake him up. Her authoritative voice announces to them: he doesn't have a fever, they already took his pulse, the other nurse was just here, come back later. Her voice lies to them: they took him to the lab to get a sample, he's with the urologist. Or just to see how they react she says: my dad is naked, he's pooping and it smells terrible, he went out to buy cigarettes, he'll be right back. The nurses don't believe her, but they also don't dare challenge her.

But she has to let the soldiers in because they're coming to fix the air-conditioning that hasn't worked in months. They bow as they cross the threshold; the doctor must be treated with the respect he deserves, as the soldier with the thick mustache declares with exaggerated diction. The other one, baby-faced, takes off his cap and nods. The Girl Twin arches her eyebrow and leaves the room with the infant hanging from her breast and the camera from her shoulder, propping the phone up with her face so she can finish her conversation. She's going, she says, to get a yogurt. The Mother follows her out and convinces her to go to the café across the street. The coffee here is just terrible, says the Mother, sighing; she never can find one to her liking. I just don't understand why your dad chose this awful hospital, she's saying as she closes the door. If she only knew, thinks Ella, if she only knew. Better she doesn't, better she goes on thinking he spent all the money on a second family, better for those two to leave. I'll stay with him and the soldiers in this place where who knows how many people were tortured to death years ago. The rooms are full of *echoes anchors curtains of smoke*. The hallways, of incomprehensible noises. The soldiers are silent as they await their orders, and Ella thinks how these two who now sport caps and boots and uniforms of useless camouflage had not even been born yet in the violent years of her childhood. She allows herself to reach out her callused hands and ask them for a favor. Since they're going to fix the problem with the air, while they're at it could they also change the fluorescent bulb on the wall? It doesn't work either. The winter afternoons are sad and gloomy. At your service, says the young conscript with the acne-eaten face, and the one with the mustache smiles ambiguously. Maybe there is no answer. Maybe the problem is something else. A problem cubed or raised to the tenth power. There are knocks at the door that then opens and lets in a third soldier with sure steps and fatigues. This one, an electrician by profession though his uniform says otherwise, concludes that those burned bulbs are from another era. A bald soldier comes in and agrees. This four-person army surrounds the shrunken Father in his bed, which they immediately pull away from the wall. The tallest one pushes it and another, who is the skinniest but has an air of authority, pulls it, and Ella begs them not to knock over the IV or tangle any cables. She pulls up her knees on the torn sofa, cornered now by her Father.

That quantic hair that was once black, that once hid the sunspots Ella sees on her Father's skull, is now just beneath the TV screen, just under the legs of two tennis players who run back and forth on the court; they slide on their tennis shoes and recover, they pound the ball, they swirl some little skirts that the camera focuses on from behind, they display their muscular thighs and shaved shins, they wipe the sweat from their foreheads on their wristbands.

Reduced by the military electricians to the minimum possible length of their bodies: Ella's knees bend in a thousand places to form impossible angles on the dilapidated sofa. The anemic Father's neck is more crooked than ever, and from that distance the rectangular TV is a *resplendent logarithmic spiral* whose volume the Father has raised with a remote control that is now the source of his only authoritative power. They are all bewitched by the screen, all admiring that overly white tennis player and the other, very black, who go on dealing each other mortal blows, brief, syncopated cries, sweaty groans that the pounding rackets can't conceal.

Never taking their eyes from the tennis players, the uniformed men uncouple the heavy base of the light attached along the wall behind the bed. It raises a cloud of *accrued years hairs wings mites*, atoms of the patients who came before the Father and that no one has bothered to vacuum. Ella breathes them in and coughs them out, disgusted, and remorsefully ponders the fact that her Father's wound is open, or closed but above all infectable, and that hospitals are high-risk zones for a sick man.

* * *

A cleaning woman is moving her mop over other people's filth while she unabashedly coughs up bronchitic phlegm. She sprays elemental particles over linoleum that's been worn by decades of disinfectant. There's a crowd of wheels and feet, of laces and plugs, of voices that hamper her work. The mop strings get tangled in the military boots, soaking them. It's the devious, damp trap that she sets for the soldiers.

* * *

And the same way they entered they take their leave, one by one, the nurse, the cleaning woman, the soldiers, until only one is left, the one with the childish face. That one stands before Ella and recites, waving some hardened hands, an incomprehensible report on the antiquated lighting system that runs through the ruinous building, the many inconveniences it's caused them, the wiring, the alternating current, the nonexistent replacement parts, the paltry public hospital budget. They've had to change another blown bulb and a switch that didn't work. He talks to her as if she were the hospital director or the head of maintenance or the head of this household where she now lives, as if she were her Father's owner or his representative. But she's nothing but an occasional daughter.

The bitter Father: that damned soldier only talked to you, like I'm just here for decoration.

The ascetic Father doesn't have the strength for the newspaper or the concentration for a novel. There's nothing to watch on TV and there's no reason to waste electricity, he says, turning off the newly repaired light.

He's not going to die, Ella decides, relieved to see him grumbling.

* * *

What the Mother on the other end of the line wants is for Ella to describe the urine in the bag or the bottle it was emptied into. She asks this unaware that the daughter is incapable of discerning shades of color. The daughter hesitates. It's not *lemon butter banana*, nor is it *honey corn caramel pineapple mustard*. Not *orange or eternal flame*. Watermelon juice? insists the Mother, adding that blood lends a lot of color. No, Ella replies, getting more entangled in the tonal varieties of yellow and red. A little more fiery.

Another glass of water? If I drink any more water, threatens the Father, I'm going to explode.

Ella would have tasted his urine to diagnose him. As a child, she compared the taste of her urine with that of her three siblings. The Twins pissed in diapers where she deposited her tongue, and the Firstborn didn't flush, as if he aspired to participate in her tongue's investigation, as if he wanted to find out how far her thirst for knowledge would go.

* * *

It's all over the news, the lung they've just transplanted into a little girl's body. An adult lung that Ella imagines suffocating in a rib cage only seven or eight years old. A child about to explode. You haven't learned anything, objects the Father. They only transplanted pieces of lung.

Ella changes the channel and what appears is the soundtrack of the streets filled with protesters. Thunderous noise, barely tolerable. She's about to change the channel again but instead sits looking at the demonstrators howling against a pension system that has condemned them to an old age of abandonment, and she wonders if they're sending her a subliminal message.

* * *

Sitting on the hard green sofa, dodging a leak that drips into a container and spatters the wall. Ella is reading the end of a biography of the paralyzed physician who is about to die, or is perhaps already dead.

A slipper swings from his toes while the Father says: you should have read that novel I recommended. She looks up in surprise because she doesn't know what he's talking about. You'll find it on the third shelf, in the sixth position left to right, the Father directs, dictating from memory the cartography of his office. And at that exact coordinate Ella finds, that night, an edition of dry and brittle pages sliced from centenary forests that went extinct ages ago. A classic wrapped in transparent plastic and covered in dust. When she opens it she sees his slightly slanted signature at the foot of a sepia page that was still white when he recorded the date, a calligraphic 05/1957. This is the book that spurred him to study medicine.

She wonders what he could have liked so much about that novel. The doctor is an arrogant toad with jumpy eyes, obsessed with the recent discovery of x-rays. He's an infamous, ironic doctor, with no pity for his patients. *Translucent tadpoles between two waters* is the phrase that distracts her. The Father is asleep. Ella will forget to ask him.

The blemish left by the asymptomatic tuberculosis he had but doesn't know when. Calcification was what that scar was called.

* * *

The tuberculosis patients of that novel inhabit high, stony peaks. The healthy people in the lower lands, the nether regions that were one single country.

* * *

It was the only country prepared for the melting poles and rising waters that were being announced. The country that had implemented a drainage system that would prevent the floods the rest of the planet would suffer. On a trip to that country below sea level, Ella had suffered an infection that came close to destroying her kidneys.

* * *

You were always one of us, ventures the jumpy-eyed doctor when he discovers that the protagonist, visiting to take care of his cousin, is also infected.

We are probably always sick and don't know it. And although as a child Ella had thought they were trying to scare her with all those stories of what a body can suffer, only later has she understood that those stories were nothing but a gloss. Because the strangest thing is to live. So much can go wrong, she thinks, looking away from her book to check the bag of urine and its changing color.

* * *

General Urology. She finds this manual on another shelf in the paternal office where she spends a few nighttime hours entertaining herself with urology. Fifth edition, 1966. The Father has noted the present of his reading in blue ink, *1967*. The Father who signs his name is twenty-seven years old. He writes his name three times:

203

on the first blank page; on the second page, under the title; and on the third, beside the table of contents.

It's strange. Her Father forbids her to write in any of the books he lends her, but these pages are underlined in the compulsive manner of a student. The Mother assures her that the textbook is hers, but perhaps only the underlining is.

Underlined and annotated books: messages that the Mother left for Ella in the future and for her husband in the past that they shared.

If they both studied that textbook, the Mother must have studied it later.

Reading notes. Slanted handwriting on a loose sheet stuck between the pages. A correction, sentences crossed out and rewritten.

1) *Abundant water*
2) *Avoid repro* (What could this mean? Is it what she's picturing?)
3) *Ingestion of vitamins and minerals*
4) *Limit milk, eliminate cheese*
5) *Acid phosphate Na or 12 4–6 g. Neutral phosphate Na or 12 2.5 g*
6) *Pyridoxine. Folic acid. > 25 mg x 30*
7) *Avoid potatoes, sweets, sweet fruit, blackberries, spinach, jell-o, cabbage, tomato, celery, beet, cocoa, tea, coffee, rhubarb.*

* * *

With more blood cells in his system, the Father would have shown more interest in the discovery of that handwritten page. He makes no effort to remember it and shows no interest at all in reconstructing the situation that might call for such a treatment. Everything has changed so much, I'm learning to forget what I learned, because that knowledge doesn't apply anymore, it's worthless. Listening to a patient's body, examining it, touching it; now the only certainty comes from machines, the eyes of machines. Medicine today isn't the same thing I studied, he adds with a yawn.

But the daughter would rather avoid the machines and those eyes that see all, the minuscule and the distant and the deep, things inaccessible to the human eye.

Feigning distraction, the daughter focuses on the oxytetracycline printed on the bottom of the page. I think that's a broad-spectrum antibiotic in the tetracycline family, right? She consults the web, the Father consults with himself, yes, yes, he says, and he thinks about it a little more. It's used to treat diseases in bees.

Because *workers drones but not queens* suffered from parasites huddled in their bodies, and from bacterial and fungal varieties that spread to those heads of theirs crowned by two antennae that were their nostrils, their heads full of eyes: compound eyes on their temples, and on their foreheads, three simple eyes. There was a virus that attacked those heads or deformed their wings and legs in a mortal paralysis.

Bees, whose extinction would occasion the end of humanity.

They didn't know stillness, not even inside the hive. Their wings beat the air to keep them aloft and carry them the hundreds of *kilometers isotopes ages* that they were capable of traveling. They tended and fed one another, they defended one another by stinging the community's enemies, they died gutted in suicide attacks. The Father let her talk, but when she paused for breath he clarified that bees weren't as communistic as they might seem. They could be cruel: a sick bee was expelled from the hive by its healthy companions, to protect the queen and the other workers.

Humans had also done this during times of worsening plagues.

* * *

Ella is digging in her pockets for change when a woman approaches carrying a little boy whose cheeks are swollen by mumps. Cramps in the parotid gland. The boy is crying. The woman hands Ella a coin, and though Ella knows there is some risk in accepting it, she rushes to slide it into the slot and grab the second coffee from the machine. She races away from the woman, skips the elevator that's always overflowing with people. She climbs the emergency-exit stairs, balancing the coffees on the landing, where she stops to catch her breath.

Nothing pleases her Father so much as seeing her arrive with that repugnant instant coffee that they drink together, every morning, in secret.

* * *

Successive messages from the Mother. Did the physical therapist come? Did the Father do his exercises? Did he walk in the hallway? If not, the muscular atrophy will be brutal.

Bones can atrophy too, Ella thinks, and then she forgets that she thought it.

* * *

His hair has grown in spite of the anemia. He pushes it forward with a comb he keeps in his pocket. He's always worn shirts with pockets and thin little combs inside them, never T-shirts, never shorts, never sneakers: he's always been a formal man, impeccable, and now he wears a robe that's open on the sides with four loose strings that leave his ribs exposed, his gray torso. The cloth reaches only to the middle of his scrawny thighs. They walk slowly, the two of them, down the hallway. The Father is stooped over as he drags his IV stand with the bag, and he zigzags like he's getting drunk on saline. His ribs poking out, his grizzled chest, the country below wrapped in white gauze, and the catheter and the liters of *juice honey hungry ants.* And the white socks that would save him from blood clots if they weren't already worn-out. If they weren't fallen down over his ankles. Ella decides not to look back when her Father bends down to pull them up.

The dreadful giggles of the nurses and young aides.

They're used to the patients' exhibitionism, writes El, remembering his recent colonoscopy. *You've seen one butt, you've seen 'em all.* Ella knows that not all asses are created equal. Or all penises. Her Father's, wrapped in cloth.

***

In the bed, the Father and the scanty public hospital robe. The Mother exclaims, impatient, could you cover yourself up a little?

***

A Father in a shower and a daughter there with him. And a dark and wrinkled hide that hangs between them, amid the curly tangle of his legs. Ella doesn't have wild hair or that paternal hide, but, when she grows up. Because everyone says that Ella is just like her Father.

***

You've got to let the doctors come in, says the Father as he finishes his coffee. In that hospital as in all hospitals there roams a troop of octogenarian doctors who know him, who were his colleagues, and there also snake through the hallways, more resolved, more anxious, talking on their cell phones, neophyte doctors who were his students. Their heads peek in the door to say, hi, how are we doing, doctor? and they give a bow and go on with their walk toward other patients, relieved it's not them in that bed. That afternoon there are three newly graduated doctors who stop by the room. In spite of the anemia and confusion, the Father recites every one of their last names, while they, who were about to identify themselves, keep their names on the tips of their tongues. The Father shows off, reeling off the *year semester eternity* when they were his students, the mistakes they made on the final exam, their grades.

* * *

At her Friend's house when the Friend was still in her last year of medical school, the Father's students would often commiserate with Ella. Their apparent pity was nothing but the prologue to a session of venting. Her Father started his classes speaking in a loud lecturer's voice, but he gradually lowered it until he was impossible to hear, even for the students sitting in the first row. Some of them had learned to read his lips as his voice evaporated. And the daughter couldn't help but smile, because she knew that paternal strategy. Ella herself used it in the classroom: when she noticed her students were distracted, she dropped a few decibels. Her students found themselves obliged to migrate to the front row and pay full attention. Or else submit to the whisper that would let them sleep. Ella was demanding on tests, just like the Father whom the aspiring doctors complained of. It wasn't just that her Father was severe on the written test and ruthless in his grading; he tended to humiliate his students on oral exams for any lack of precision. For a forgotten detail. For excess information and lack of understanding. For not conceiving of the organism as a complex system of signs. For not listening carefully to the list of symptoms. Her Father reminded them that they, every one of them, were responsible for lives and would pay for them if they made a mistake. Error, however, was written into the brain. To err is human, difficult as it was to admit. Only the 404 error belonged to the machine.

* * *

The image of the sliced brain as Ella cuts a cauliflower in half and pulls apart its stalks to *boil mash spilt milk* with cream and salt. Its thick nerve system, its nearly gray white.

* * *

One day she would hear him say that he'd had to learn to let everyone make their own mistakes. By then the Father was retired.

Another day he said that people live better when they don't remember their suffering. I'm learning to rid my head of the past, he said. His forgetful daughter agreed.

* * *

The stern doctor who was her Father never mentioned his own mistakes or the deaths accumulated in the folds of his brain. His own mother had perished in an operating room, and he wasn't able to stop it. Are you allergic to any medications? the anesthesiologist had asked her. No, replied the old lady, full of forgetting. Her memorious son, newly graduated from medical school, would have corrected her, would have explained that she had already suffered two reactions to dipyrone. One slight. Another moderate. The third dose would be the last. Suicide by distraction.

And there was another negligent death he wished he had prevented and that he never managed to forget, because his memory wouldn't allow it. And the Firstborn's wrath. And his daughter's unbearable forgiveness.

* * *

She observes him sitting at a table, without *stethoscope hair gel full-color mustache*, not moving his lips. Ella brings up her biological mother, asks for the first time if she was the one who provoked her mother's death, or if the aspirin produced the fatal hemorrhage, or if it was the combination of daughter and drug. The Father shakes his head without raising it, as if that was where he carried the weight of his guilt. They accelerated your mother's labor, he murmured, but they overdid it with the hormones.

They'd induced a chemical death with her consent.

The Twins weren't induced, added the Father in a mournful murmur, and neither was your brother, they were all birthed slowly.

* * *

Ella was certain that it was better to have been her Father's daughter than his student, much as she would have been his best pupil. Ella. Not the Twins, and definitely not the Firstborn, who never hid his contempt for the medical profession.

I always thought you would go into medicine, said the Father, resigned but obstinate: he invariably returned to this question that had been resolved ages ago and that Ella could no longer answer. But the Father's usual monologue took a detour: in the end, though, you did become a doctor, the only one in the family. You're the doctor, replied the annoyed daughter. No, the Father contradicted her.

Medical doctors had only bachelor's degrees, to call them doctors was an etymological aberration.

She was etymologically a doctor, but behind his yellow-toothed smile stretched the shadow of a request. When would she let him read that dissertation he had financed? And he gazed at her as though probing her, and Ella held that hard, eighty-year-old gaze, those extinguished eyes, and maybe she quickly blinked a couple of times. It's just a dissertation, it's full of mistakes, she replied, trying to compose the crack in her voice, I'd rather you read it when it's edited and ready for publication.

Her Father agreed, but Ella knew he would ask again; plus, she added, you're not going to understand a bit of it, dad, it's pages and pages of cosmic equations.

* * *

The Father lifts the catheter tube to examine the bag full of *lemonade mustard dandelions*. A grimace of intense pain crosses his face, wrinkles it all except for the lips that stretch in an acidic smile. Her Father doubles up in pain. Are you all right? Ella knows something's off there inside him, and the Father knows it too. Fine, he *lies sweats pants twists*. He blurts out that there are clots trapped in the tube and that's why he's gathering it up, bending it like a hose, siphoning his own urine back into his bladder, trying to remove the blockage of dried blood that's causing his spasms. Look, look! The catheter fills with dark clots and Ella looks without wanting to look, pretending to look, turning her eyes away but looking at what inhabits her Father's insides. Blood of her blood moves down through the tube toward the vermilion bag while her Father makes faces in extraordinary pain. I'm getting the nurse, announces the daughter, hearing her Father behind her say, no, no need, he can fix this himself, and Ella hesitates, stops, splits into two to observe this scene from outside, a scene she's witnessed before. The Father unconscious from pain.

* * *

Her Father appeared in the past, inserting a long tube into Ella's stomach to remove the kerosene that she had swallowed. Though it was dangerous and forbidden, the Father had sucked out all the fuel with his mouth.

He punished her later. Then he read her another forgotten story.

Now her Father wanted to suck out the clots of his own death.

* * *

The sun was setting and then it was night. And that night Ella returns to the study and to the pages of *General Urology*. That night she starts to read them, to highlight them over what's already been highlighted. That night she turns off the light and then turns it back on. That night she leaves the bed that used to be hers and still is when she's in it, and she goes into the bathroom she once shared with the Twins and tries to urinate, but can't. That night she goes back to the bedroom shivering because it's deathly cold in that house she no longer knows except for its smells, and that's why she opens the closet and finds herself in the stagnant scent of another time, in the slow air of the past. She breathes in those coats still hanging there like suicides waiting to be identified.

She slips her hands quickly into the pockets. One by one into each pocket, looking for lost pieces of her Father.

* * *

Her Actor friend who is no longer an actor comes to eat with Ella. So many soldiers, he whispers into her ear, looking around him at all the conscripts. They're really beautiful, these boys. His eyes slide slowly over *ears buttons lips reinforced zippers* that could open quickly. Yes, Ella says, they may be beautiful, she says, and young, she says, but don't forget they're soldiers. Tell me about you instead. And the Actor chooses to talk about his urinary problems: the narrowing of his urethra, the iron rod they stick into it to dilate it. The Actor knows he has to subject himself to this procedure that violates his privacy every five years, but he waits until not a drop can get out, until he feels himself bursting. Ella imagines him standing there naked with the iron wire hanging out, the urine running down it. She orders a soda, he orders a blond beer, Ella thinks her friend is doing this on purpose. Instead of sitting, the soldiers carry their lunches and their sodas and their coffees off to who knows where. And now? Ella asks, out of politeness, praying he won't give her more than a summary. All good? A last orangish flash of dreck has just peeked between the clouds over the mountains, and the yellow leaves shine, autumnal. I'm too fat, he says, I spend too many hours sitting in the office, sitting with my gut out. My penis cramps up.

* * *

Sonda means catheter, and in some other language it means sound. And it's music that she hears when they remove her Father's and the urine falls into the metal container under the sheets.

* * *

The massage therapist is the urologist's daughter, she specializes in reanimation. That's what Ella texts to El that night. El replies with question marks. She dictates another text and sends it, realizing too late that she forgot to change the keyboard language. The system goes crazy. *Dónde estás debes desde llegado ya es tarde está Sofe es vistas Station.* She dictates again, it's wrong again, *si es una experta en encanten empieces.* Finally she changes the keyboard and dictates: *She's an expert in incontinence and impotence.*

An odd specialty, El responds, and Ella thinks it's an ironic remark that could have come from the Firstborn.

That long-haired massage therapist rubs him from the tips of his toes up to his shins to stimulate his circulation.

Ella leaves them alone. She lets her Father cheat on her with someone else's daughter.

* * *

Mother and daughter catch up to the urologist in the middle of a hallway to confirm that he'll sign the release papers after removing the stitches. Your daughter is so nice, Ella says, just to say something. To say something else, the Mother also celebrates the odd specialty, and she adds with a smile, I could use some reanimation myself.

* * *

The night before it was barely a flush, now it's full-on fever and a series of questions. A gram of paracetamol.

Ella is waiting for the coffee to come out of the machine when she hears someone behind her. She clutches the machine, prepares herself. Betrayal always comes from behind. Stabbed in the back. It's the urologist, who's just rescinded the discharge. The blood panel is irregular. The white blood cells indicate an infection somewhere in the body, though they don't know where. He doesn't think it's cause for concern, but a call comes from the lab that indicates otherwise. An in-hospital infection. The fearful drug-resistant infection.

They're looking for an infectious-disease specialist, which this poor hospital doesn't have.

* * *

Every three seconds someone dies from a generalized infection that goes by the name septicemia. Her Father: he was weak but not confused, he had fever but not chills, his breathing was regular, his skin wasn't covered with spots. That didn't mean that he couldn't take a sudden turn for the worse. Time was against him.

* * *

Two lukewarm coffees and five floors up the Father declares he's going home. Hand me my clothes and wait for me outside, he commands, but the drill sergeant his daughter has become doesn't move. She sits on the sofa that by now has her bony imprint and she reminds him that at home he'll just be in another bed, and when it comes to beds, better to be in one in the hospital. Even if it's this crumbling place. The Father and his scornful expression. His flayed-rabbit slippers beneath the bed.

Pants hanging in the closet. A shirt newly rescued from the dry cleaner. It would be a matter of standing up, putting on socks and shoes, tying a tie, getting into a swift wheelchair, and taking his leave: that's what he wants and it falls to Ella to stop him, because who knows when the Mother will turn up to block his way.

* * *

When El got those sudden, ferocious fevers, Ella applied cold cloths, because that was the recommendation. She was afraid of the way El's temperature could shoot up and stay high, afraid of what it could provoke in his brain, *cook it melt it turn it to mush*. She would worry that this time he really had caught malaria or dengue fever or cholera or whatever other plague fermented down in those excavations. Ella wet towels with cold water and convinced him that was the only way to bring his fever down, and El shivered on the mattress. No more, please, no more, Electroshock, he howled, but Ella told him to be quiet and take it.

The cloths shouldn't be that cold, the Father reproached her later, just lukewarm. The way a fever nose-dives from the freezing cold can be terrible.

But cold was what had settled in between them. Love, like a fever, had eventually cooled. Ella had asked him not to call her again, and she'd thought he would howl back like a beaten dog, but El put up no resistance. It's better this way, he murmured sorrowfully.

* * *

Having knowledge didn't mean you acted in accordance with it.

If you were your treating physician, dad, would *you* release you with that fever? Testily, the Father got out his stethoscope and put it over his heart to see if the rising fever had accelerated it. He fell asleep to the steady rhythm of his own heartbeat.

That hollow little organ behind its shield of bone wasn't always a metaphor.

* * *

Clock story. Lacking a second hand, the ancients measured time with heartbeats, never thinking that an arrhythmia could alter the calculation.

Because the days passed *slow heavy elephant heart* and because she lost track of time, Ella was surprised that the athletic Firstborn was now a somewhat hunched-over man who walked through the door with difficulty. And that the Boy Twin had a beard and wore patent leather shoes. The Girl Twin had arrived with a maternal air, pushing a stroller that wouldn't fit through the doorway, and Ella realized that her sister, too, was no longer a child. The Mother was an old woman now, and she'd been barely forty when the Father, who had some years on her, starred in the commercial for blood-thinning aspirin. The dead time of the hospital now offered them a chance to go back to that commercial that constituted, always, a disputed memory, an opportunity for a fight. The Firstborn blurted out his words contemptuously, he'd never seen the Father on-screen. Ella raised her eyebrows and said she *had* seen him, wrapped in his white coat and surrounded by other doctors. The Boy Twin corrected her, the Father was alone and he was standing, but how could the Boy Twin know that, he'd been only a boy. There was no one else, the Boy Twin insisted, and the Girl Twin nodded, emphasizing her double chin. Alone and very serious, that's how dad was, and the Boy Twin added: he said short and solemn sentences in a low voice, with no expression on his face, like a fixed image with a voice-over.

* * *

The keynote address. Her Father spoke about the evolution of the catheters that snaked through veinous and arterial channels, removing accumulated plaque on the way to the heart. It was a story of small tubes that made their way through the body with an inflatable balloon on the tip. The Father showed drawings on slides, or maybe they were transparencies that he placed on a light box and projected onto the wall. In front of an auditorium full of specialists. In front of his family. A chance for the Mother to show off that crowd of children, her own and those on loan. She made them dress up but they never had formal clothes, so instead they wore their school uniforms without the insignia. Except the Firstborn, who bowed out with the excuse of some sports event, so he wouldn't have to applaud his Father.

The Father's voice grew gradually softer, until an old doctor begged him from the audience, professor, speak up.

* * *

Her thermodynamics professor rose up and eclipsed that memory: that obsession with *ducts tubes enemas catheters* must be a thing with shy teachers.

* * *

Incompetent. That's the Father's verdict on the eminent infectious-disease specialist brought in from a private clinic to attend to this emergency. He's just decided that the patient won't be going any farther than the ultrasound room, where they'll be able to see if there's a swarm of bacteria beneath the wound. The Father had mentioned that when the stitches were removed he saw a drop of serous liquid emerge. Ooze. Seep. Exude. It's nothing, he'd said, knowing perfectly well that the fever was there.

The microscope would have the last word.

* * *

The lights turn on, the bag of urine shines like a fallen sun.

*　*　*

The Father had been wheeled through the open halls of that ancient hospital, overhung patios, buckets set out to collect the dirty water dripping from the ceilings, walls cracked by earthquakes, tiles come up in the corners; in some secret room they were draining his urine, dirty with anonymous bacteria that soon they'd be able to name. In the meantime the Mother was waiting for him in his cold room, wrapped in a blanket she'd brought from home, and she'd plugged her phone into the wall. The clock marked seconds on the screen, hateful minutes, a too-slow hour or maybe more. And Ella was killing time before returning when she received a message from her Father's phone, but it was the Mother who was writing on the borrowed device. Her phone had disappeared. *How could it be stolen, mom, weren't you right there? Couldn't you have left it somewhere else?* Because every time the Mother loses something she thinks she's been robbed. The Mother responds instantly to dispel the daughter's doubts. *People are constantly coming in and out*, and she fills the screen with furious exclamation points. *They must have come in quietly. Maybe I fell asleep a couple of minutes*, she writes, *I'm exhausted, I'm sick of this den of thieves.*

God has sent me this torture to try my patience, says the Mother, blowing the locks of hair that fall over her eyes. Only when she wants to blame someone does the Mother invoke God, remorseless.

*　*　*

Portrait of stoicism. The Father is wrapped in thought the way he used to be in clouds of cigarette smoke. The Father sweeping up crumbs on the plate with a finger, crushing them, gathering them to lift them to his mouth. The Father spooning chicken broth with an imperturbable expression. The Mother's funereal face as she watches him eat like a bird. The Father tapping his hard nails against his teeth like a woodpecker. The Father winding his watch and writing down what he will do once they set him free from the hospital, though his agenda will never return his lost days.

The Father complains about nothing while the Mother does the opposite, never stops complaining.

The Mother works without a break, as if instead of working she were escaping that public hospital she will never return to.

* * *

And is bone boy coming to see you? Who knows, replies the daughter, shrinking from the truth. Everything has twisted up between them. El hasn't called again and doesn't reply to the messages she sends, much as he *receives reads tears them into a thousand pieces*, and Ella is afraid he's thrown his phone against a door, that he's shattered the screen, but she knows that's not what has happened.

Emptiness has opened up between them, and there is no filling it.

* * *

She watches a vitamin dissolve in water. Rising bubbles that burst, birthing an effervescent galaxy that Ella will swallow.

* * *

How much antibiotics are they giving you, dad? I don't know. You didn't ask? No, I didn't ask, but Ella knows he's lying. They must be giving me a very high dosage, says the Father then, and he adds irritably, they're using machine guns to kill mosquitoes. That way they wipe out all the mosquitoes at once, Ella replies. Right, agrees the

Father, raising his voice as if rage had a tonic effect on his vocal cords. And that way they're killing me.

Just then Ella squashes another of the hospital's promiscuous mosquitoes. Its wings are crushed against the wall, stuck there with the blood, *fresh lethal golden staphylococcus*, that the mosquito sucked from the Father. Because mosquitoes have hearts but not blood, Ella remembers, gazing at the bloody trail of her Father stretching over the cracked paint. It's a constellation of stains.

It was an instantaneous death, this time. Other times her slap manages only to knock down the mosquito, and it's left agonizing, feet in the air, convulsing.

* * *

The report from the microscope: there are almost no bacteria in the serous liquid. The Father was right: they used machine guns to wipe out a slight infection. The strong antibiotic has an immediate effect, and the Father breaks infected water through the wound. Soaking *bandage robe sheets hours newspapers*.

And yet, they don't release him.

And her Father, meanwhile, ages.

* * *

After emerging from confinement, the patient must start to recover from his recovery. The Father, sunk in his hole, waits for that moment.

* * *

Didn't habitable planets ever interest you? asks the Father, not asking the question Ella would have expected. Ella smiles sadly, shaking her head and then nodding, because she had considered the subject but then abandoned it, like she did almost everything. But she knows the cosmologists were hard at work finding alternative planets, that there were already a hundred and nineteen candidates, though only ten were the same size and temperature as earth. Some people claimed to have found water on a planet in another solar system called trappist. And? interrupts the Father, and Ella explains that that system is forty light-years away, 9.5 billion kilometers multiplied by forty, and the Father purses his lips in disappointment and raises the newspaper to end the conversation, but then he lays it back on the bed and asks about the underground saltwater lake they've just discovered on the red planet. Yes, Ella admits, there's a lake under the ice, but we don't know how much water is there. And Mars is millions of miles from here, seven months in a shuttle, she says, her eyes fixed on the window.

Some people believed they were adrift on a great space rock spinning in circles, left to its fate; those were people who aspired only not to leave orbit, not to collide with another, similar rock, or the sun.

* * *

It's a particularly cold morning, even for the merciless winters of the preterit country that is starting to become, again, slowly, her country of the present. The Father has just been released, he's sitting in a chair rolling toward the exit. The temperature is low and the humidity high, but the Father refuses to bundle up. Ella's teeth chatter in spite of the scarf and the coat brought from the north pole, and the umbrella she opens to keep the rain from pissing down on them. She says good-bye to the nurses in their thin military uniforms, wondering when she'll have to return with her Father to that insalubrious hospital. Because his recovery is a datum only of the now, and his survival now doesn't mean he won't die the next time. It's a question of probability, and probability is at the heart of science.

It will rain again and clear up again, the perfect blue mountains will again be visible, snowy down to their feet. A clean sun will ignite among the watery clouds, filling the large window, and Ella will sit beside that Father centuries older, sicker, beside him Ella, *old hook-nosed mustached bitter*, a useless lie still stuck in her throat.

* * *

Waiting for the taxi that still hasn't come, Ella thinks she should tell him while she still can. Tell him how she never wrote that dissertation. How she missed the deadline to turn it in. How that morning she'd received a letter from the university informing her of her definitive expulsion. There's no turning back now and she should feel liberated, but she thinks she's more a prisoner than ever, with that *letter life sentence scaphoid screws* still in her inbox. Her heart shrank, turned cold when she read it.

To say dad as the downpour intensifies. To hear a decrepit voice say, did you say something? To reply, aren't you cold, dad? and repeat the question over the rain in a broken voice. To hear the Father whisper, is something wrong? as if he knew without needing to turn his head toward her, standing behind the wheelchair. No one can hear them. No, dad, says Ella, and her tongue is a hiss, her voice a reed soaked by the storm, and then she pronounces a clumsy, that's not true, dad, I'm not sure, but the words end there. The Father stretches his elderly eyes toward Ella as if seeking her dilated pupils in the umbrella's gloom. Yes, agrees the Father, nothing is certain, and that's the genuine truth.

The problem was never the theory of physics, much as her evidence was weak and her approach speculative. The problem was, or is, and she rushes her words because the Father tries to interrupt her, that the mathematical proof was killing me. Ella had ended up accepting that she cared only about what she didn't understand, what couldn't be seen, the conjectural, fumbling her way through the dark room of the cosmos. Not putting her eye to telescopes so powerful they let you read an open newspaper on the moon. And the Father shakes his head as though asking her to be quiet but Ella can't be quiet and she tells him, agonizing, that she tried but couldn't do it and she spent her Father's last cent. Your savings, your retirement.

I already knew, murmurs the Father, shivering in the cold. And he pauses before finishing, because he thinks he sees a taxi in the distance and he raises a hand to flag it down. You're not a good liar, *hija*, and, moving from the present tense to past he adds: You blinked a lot every time I asked you. You blinked the way your mom blinked when she lied to me. The same quick blinking, the same flash in your eyes.

* * *

She wanted to tell him she'd read in a book, not long ago, that one who listened carefully didn't need to see. She wanted to tell him that that line had shaken her, it had stung, she'd coughed convulsively and then closed her eyes and understood something she couldn't put into words, and that's why she didn't tell him.

* * *

They're still on the sidewalk, between lines of parked cars, the two of them. Abandoned, the two of them. Ella pushes the wheelchair farther from the hospital to see if she can find a car that will get them out of those wet streets. Then she realizes there's a transportation strike going on in the city. The metro trains, buses, taxis, all those drivers standing downtown, holding signs. Things are a mess here, says the Father when Ella reminds him, too much of a mess for me. Customs strike, transportation strike, and there's one at the architects' association announced for Monday, teachers on Thursday, and another student protest, then immigrants, then hundreds of women who've been raped and beaten and murdered in this country. And bank robberies, falling bridges, droughts, political troubles, corrupt and shameless politicians. And it's not just here, says the Father. It's everywhere, in every country. It's incredible that earth is still spinning in one piece. How many seconds are we from global catastrophe, half a minute? he says, raising his wounded-bird voice. What's the latest from the doomsday clock? But Ella doesn't reply, she can't speak, this Father still short on red blood cells but full of energy, this resuscitated Father is saying that the future is the color of ants, and he'd like to escape to another planet.

We should fix up this planet, not take off to another one where we'd repeat the same mistakes. The same mistakes, repeats the Father, what mistakes could we repair? Which one would you start with? he asks, staring off into space, closing his eyes, *dreamy anemic lamb to the slaughter.*

Rekindled by the wind he adds, you have nothing now, not even that man of yours, right? The scientist you lived with? And I can't support you. What are you going to do? What do you want to do? Ella looks at him with emptied eyes, as if she's disappeared inside herself, as if she were drowning. Cut and run with you? and she raises her eyebrows. Off to another planet? and she stammers, her voice is many voices, her question is *nervous nebulous shooting short circuit of stars.*

It's a deal, says the Father, seeing sparks around his daughter, his daughter touched by the light. Plus, he says, you owe me that, I'll need you on that trip. You're the expert on the great beyond.

LINA MERUANE is an award-winning Chilean writer of short stories and five novels, including *Seeing Red*, winner of the prestigious Sor Juana Inés de la Cruz Prize (Mexico) and the Premio Valle-Inclán (UK). She is also the author of several nonfiction books, including *Viral Voyages: Tracing AIDS in Latin America*. She has also received the Anna Seghers Prize and grants from the Guggenheim Foundation and the National Endowment for the Arts, and she was a DAAD Artist in Residence in Berlin. She teaches global cultures and creative writing at New York University.

MEGAN MCDOWELL has translated many of the most important Latin American writers working today, including Samanta Schweblin and Alejandro Zambra. Her translations have won the English PEN award and the Premio Valle-Inclán and have been nominated three times for the International Booker Prize. Her short-story translations have been featured in the *New Yorker*, the *Paris Review*, *Tin House*, *McSweeney's*, and *Granta*, among other publications. She is the recipient of a Literature Award from the American Academy of Arts and Letters. She lives in Santiago, Chile.

The text of *Nervous System* is set in Century Old Style Std.
Book design by Rachel Holscher.
Composition by Bookmobile Design and Digital Publisher
Services, Minneapolis, Minnesota.
Manufactured by McNaughton & Gunn on acid-free,
100 percent postconsumer wastepaper.